Marina Eshl

A Horse-Worthy Name

Special thanks to:

Olga Prominski

for translation

Julia Bandura

Lesly Bolen

Rita Svatos

for their help with editing.

Though Timothy had already finished all his work in the stables, he kept hanging around and looking for something else to do. Anything at all. He really didn't want to leave - the smell of horses and the hay had completely intoxicated him.

He was certainly taken with this farm. Even its main house, so big and cumbersome, seemed quite comfortable to him now.

You would really like it here, JK. Just look at all these amazing horses. These people don't even realize what unbelievable horses they have here.

Forcing himself, Timothy picked up the bucket and slowly headed for the door. The thoughtful gaze of the horses followed him along.

A taxi pulled up to the front porch. A girl jumped out and let out a happy shriek.

"Grandma!!! Here I am!!!"

Another granddaughter. Timothy smiled. *Exactly how many do the owners have? Looks like this one is another 'troublemaker' rather than 'girl', huh, JK?*

"My little Princess! You're here," Grandma exclaimed as she squeezed her treasure in the tightest of hugs.

"Grandma! Stop it! I'm not little anymore!"

"Oh no, you're not! You're all grown up! So tall!"

Wow, JK, nobody talks in this house, they all yell, that's for sure.

"Tim!" called Grandma.

He turned abruptly and stared at her questioningly.

"You're Tim, right? Tim Miller?"

He nodded.

"Very well, then," Grandma seemed glad that her memory hadn't failed her. "I couldn't find Sean. Would you mind taking the luggage into the house?"

Timothy put the bucket down.

"Well, Grandma, is anyone else here yet?!" exclaimed the 'troublemaker' Princess, although as soon as she saw Timothy, she stumbled over her words, stopping and turning beet red.

"Almost everyone is here. Melissa, Melinda, Melanie and all three of the boys. Emily and Eric are over at the McGregors'. They're expecting your friend Vince any day now. As soon as he heard you were coming, he changed all his plans and decided to come here instead."

"Grandma!" hissed the poor embarrassed Princess and, trying her best to avoid looking at Timothy, rushed into the house. She tripped over the bucket on her way. The bucket rolled loudly across the yard.

Timothy finished bringing the last of the things in.

"He's our new employee."

"Why, Grandma?! Isn't Sean enough? I'm here to help out too."

"Well, Sean's getting old and can't carry the same load on his shoulders. Besides, he's absolutely delighted with this Tim!"

"Where should I put this?" Timothy asked.

"You can leave it right here. Come on, I'll introduce you. This is my granddaughter Sylvia."

Timothy greeted her with a nod and went to search the yard for the bucket.

"Great guy, just a little on the quiet side. The horses adore him."

"What an idiot I am! What's he going to think now! An idiot and a klutz! Why do we need him here anyway? Nobody ever asked my opinion," thought Sylvia and felt so embarrassed. "He definitely noticed my awkwardness. He probably imagined all sorts of things. And I didn't even get a good look at him. Why, why am I always so easily thrown off! He's just a guy! Why can't I be more like Melissa! All calm, smiling and dignified!"

Sylvia didn't stay upset for very long. Her Grandfather was already rushing in to greet her. He was limping and carrying a cane. His eyes were shining with joy. He hugged her tight with one arm. She pressed her face into the stubble on his face.

"Sylvia! You're finally here. You need to stop getting so tall; you'll be taller than all your dates soon!"

Sylvia never got upset over Grandpa's teasing.

Did you see her, JK? A real baby horse. Gets tangled up in her own two feet. She is a 'troublemaker' for sure.

At first, everything was exactly as it seemed. In the very early hours a loud "Good Morning!" woke the entire house. Sylvia greeted everyone, but not Timothy. He heard her loud foot stomping, her stumbling into every wall and her loud indignations over every bump.

"The clumsy Princess is up." Sean smiled gently.

Next, she went to fly kites in the company of the other 'troublemakers' - the three younger grandsons - who were finally staying out of trouble if only for the time being.

I wonder if she brought those kites with her or had them stashed away here ahead of time, JK.

The 'troublemakers'' pranks got even trickier now that they had a worthy leader. Still, the others in the house could breathe a sigh of relief, especially Grandma. At least, now the boys had someone to look after them.

***

Melissa, the oldest and the prettiest of the granddaughters, decided to throw a party. Guests, music, lots of noise. Timothy preferred to hang out quietly at the stables, where he always seemed to find something to do. Suddenly all of the girls, including Sylvia, burst in.

"Quiet!" laughed Melissa. "Saddle up and take off! Next time, they'll pay more attention to us! They call themselves gentlemen..."

All the girls burst into laughter.

"Who let you take the horses out at night?" Timothy asked stepping out of the dark.

The girls jumped up frightened.

"Nobody!" Melanie was the first one to come to her senses as she added, "We're allowed."

"As long as we are accompanied by an adult," Sylvia explained under her cousins mocking glances.

"Who's the adult here?" Timothy was smiling.

They invite a bunch of guests and then ditch them - there's female logic at work, JK. Well, it wouldn't hurt the horses to go for a ride.

"Alright, let's go then."

Timothy led them down a wide riverside path free of any obstacles. A starry night. Full bright moon. And the quiet splashing of the river. The girls giggled a little and got quiet. It was beautiful. Just like a fairy tale.

Sylvia was glancing sideways at Timothy and thinking, "Grandma had mentioned that he was twenty-one. Very mature, like Melissa. Except he looks younger. Or maybe it just seems that way." She wondered why he was going along with their prank. She thought, "Was it because of one of the cousins? Anyway, why am I always thinking about boys? About Tim, about Oscar and Vince. When is Vince finally going to get here?" The thing was, she had actually changed all her plans once she found out that he was going to spend the summer here. What if Vince changed his mind?

***

How awesome is it to be grown-up and independent? To be twenty-one, JK. Well, I've worked hard, now it's time to play hard, right? Timothy nodded to himself and opened the door in great anticipation of music, beer, and friendly girls. Everything was just as he had expected. The music was loud. Beer of any choice. Possibly, something even stronger. But he didn't manage to get around to the girls.

"Tim? Tim Miller?"

He didn't recognize Sylvia right away. He was staring down at the girl, trying to understand who was tugging at his sleeve and making him spill his beer.

"I'm lost!"

"What?!" He was now yelling over the music. He put down his glass and dragged her outside into the hall.

"Where is the bathroom?"

One look at her pale face and puffed out cheeks was enough for him to grab the nearest garbage can and stick it right under her nose. Sylvia was so embarrassed. It was awful to be standing here with her face stuck into a garbage can. On the other hand, she thought, how great it was that she found someone she knew!

Timothy listened to her long and confusing explanation about tagging along with Melissa, who had asked Ted to look after her while Melissa herself snuck out with Eric, and how she ended up losing Ted in the crowd. She'd been looking for him or for Melissa for the past hour. And she didn't know what to do - call Grandma at home to pick her up? It was so late and, well, she didn't really want to... But Sylvia never said a word to him about how petrified she was being lost in the rowdy crowd.

"Why did you drink alcohol?" Timothy grumbled.

Sylvia got quiet and hung her head low. How could she explain this to him? How could she explain to him that she had to grab the opportunity to get a taste of the grown up life? It was too much to resist. Melissa would have made a laughingstock out of her.

"You think you can manage riding without falling off?" He pointed to his old motorcycle parked on the street and scowled at her. "Leave the garbage can here."

Timothy had to stop his Harley because Sylvia was banging on his back with her fist. She quickly jumped off but didn't manage to get away and threw up right onto the road. And all over his jacket. But at this point she didn't care. Let him hate her forever. Tomorrow she'd pack up and leave, not even having seen Vince.

Timothy took off his jacket and tried to wipe it off on the grass. He ended up going over to dip it in the river.

"Come here, wash up. Just don't fall into the water."

He was laughing at her, wasn't he? The water smelled of algae. Her mouth had a nasty aftertaste. "What a fool I am," Sylvia thought.

Timothy handed her his flask. She grabbed it, noticed that he was looking and quickly rinsed her mouth. Heaven forbid he'd think she was too good for his water, she was just a slow thinker, that's all.

On the way home Sylvia was daydreaming about how things could be quite different. This could be her date. Tim could be her boyfriend and they were, naturally, being chased.

Timothy walked Sylvia to the house. She hesitated at the door.

"You know, I don't want to wake my Grandma. So she won't see me, um... like this. My window is open. Could you give me a lift? The rest I can climb myself."

He looked up.

"The banging will be pretty loud if you fall down. I was the one to cover the porch roof with that sheet metal."

And just like that, he disappeared. Sylvia was confused. Just as quickly he reappeared dragging a ladder.

"Thanks, thanks so much."

She climbed in the window.

Well, that was fun, JK, wasn't it? Remember the first time you and I got wasted? What kind of crap did we drink that time? We were idiots too. Timothy leaned the ladder against the barn wall.

"Melissa!" Sylvia remembered drifting into sleep. "I forgot all about her and she's going to be looking for me."

***

"Good morning!" A loud greeting filled the stables.

Timothy turned around, nodded, sniffed the air and questioningly raised his eyebrows at Sylvia.

"Thank you so much. I am so sorry about what happened yesterday. I won't do it again." She rambled on and on with her prepared speech.

"What did you wash your face with?" He interrupted.

"Oh, that." Sylvia sighed in embarrassment. "Melissa is getting back at me. For having to look for me and not finding me and all that. She did my make-up yesterday. So I would look older. And now she won't give me anything to take it off with. Water doesn't work. I even had to try some gasoline." She was whispering in despair.

"I see!" Timothy went back to work trying hard not to laugh out loud.

Sylvia waited around a little while and left.

"Tim! Tim! Come see me for a second!" Grandma was calling from the porch.

Timothy walked up the steps to the porch, stopped to think for a moment, took off his rubber boots and approached his boss.

"Grandma, may I go to my room?" Sylvia's head dropped.

"You sit down."

Sylvia put her head down into her palms, shook it so the hair would fall down to cover her face. She'd gone into hiding.

"I have to thank you, Tim. I hear you helped this troublemaker out of quite an adventure. Next time, though I hope there won't be a next time, you hear me, Sylvia?, don't be afraid to call me. I won't punish you too harshly." Grandma's voice filled the entire yard.

Timothy managed to notice that there wasn't any more make-up on Sylvia's face. Melissa must have taken pity on her at last and given her something to take it off with. Or Sylvia must have found some other chemical to remove it.

"My granddaughter ruined your night off. And by the way, Sean is very happy with your work. He still can't believe that you have no experience working with horses! Why don't you take the day off and go enjoy yourself?"

Timothy shrugged and looked at Grandma, surprised.

"Why don't you go check out Toronto? You're not from here, right? There're lots of things to do for fun there. Or, you could just go into town. Whatever you'd like to do."

"Can I take your granddaughter along to show me around the city?" Timothy himself was surprised with his question.

"Melissa?" Grandma also sounded surprised.

"No, Sylvia."

Sylvia squealed in delight and jumped up. "Oh, please, Grandma!"

"Alright then. But be sure to come back no later than eleven." Grandma stopped to think. "Tim, why don't you take the pickup? The one you and Sean use for everything. You know where the keys are."

Timothy nodded and headed for the stables.

***

Sylvia was thinking, "It must be great to be so grown-up. He's got holes in his socks and he couldn't care less. I would have died of embarrassment in his place. Oh, but he's asked me on a date! Well, almost a date. What's the weather going to be like? Could I wear the pink shirt? No, the blue one is better. Where is he going to take me? If I asked him right now where he was thinking of going, would I seem too desperate? But if I ask him later, how will I know what to wear?"

"No way!" Melinda said.

"You certainly have interesting taste." Melissa teased.

"You don't say. I think he looks like James Dean..." Melanie sighed longingly.

"You think everyone looks like James Dean!" Melissa laughed.

"You're just jealous of our Princess," Melinda argued. "I bet you're wondering why he didn't ask you!"

Melissa didn't say a word back. But she did go out of her way to show that she was way too good for all this. The cousins started busily inspecting Sylvia's wardrobe. There seemed to be absolutely nothing that suited the occasion. On they went to inspect their own closets.

Sylvia lucked out that the girls had left the house early in the morning, but only after making sure that she was all equipped for her date. Sylvia already regretted bringing them into the loop. What a ruckus they raised! And what if Tim Miller heard everything and decided that she was paying way too much attention to his invitation? Sylvia looked at herself in the mirror and gasped. It was one thing to have a mark on your forehead - that could be covered up with some hair. But what to do with the rest of it?!

Timothy styled spiked hair. He was ready. He drove the old pickup up to the porch. Waited a little. Honked the horn. Nobody. He had heard lots of traipsing around and shouting a half hour ago. Sylvia was definitely getting ready.

He knocked. She opened the door a crack.

"I can't." Sylvia was whispering. "Please, forgive me, but I really can't."

He stopped the door from shutting. Sylvia tried to run away. It took him two large steps to catch up to her and grab her by the shoulder. She turned away and exhaled:

"I can't!"

"Why?"

With a deep sigh she turned her cheek so he could see.

"Well?"

"I'd rather stay home. I can't go like this. What would people think? I really wanted to, believe me. This is my first date ever. And..."

"Does it hurt?"

She shook her head through the tears.

"I'm going to feel so stupid. Everyone looking at me. It will be just awful. I really did want to go. Maybe, we could have even kissed good night. Like in the movies. And now everything is ruined."

More crazy nonsense of the same kind followed.

Timothy stood in quiet disbelief.

Could a few pimples on a cheek really make one that hysterical? Oh my God, JK.

"Listen." Suddenly he had an idea that could save his day off. "Let's go someplace where there are no people. We don't have to go to the city."

"But where to?"

"The beach?"

"There's a ton of people there."

"We'll find an empty one."

"I'll be right there! Let me get my things! Just give me fifteen minutes!"

Timothy just went to get his swimming trunks, since he already had them handy. But Sylvia managed to change completely: shorts, dark sunglasses. And she was dragging along a load of bags.

A large golden lab quickly caught on that they were off on an adventure and started wagging his tail in anticipation.

"No, Gypsy King, stay home." Sylvia sounded stern.

The dog insisted.

"Alright, try telling him then." She nodded her head in Timothy's direction.

Gypsy King leaned his heavy paws into Timothy's shoulders and barked with a deafening strength. Timothy laughed and opened the door. The Labrador didn't have to be asked twice.

"Where do you want to go?" Timothy handed Sylvia the map.

She ran her finger across the eastern coast of Huron and went on explaining. There's Wasaga Beach, there's another beach.

"What about right here?" Timothy pushed aside a curious furry nose and pointed his finger further west.

"I don't know, never been there."

"Shall we find out?"

"It's at least three hours away, no less."

Timothy shrugged his shoulders and started the car. The engine gave a sneeze.

"What if the engine stalls? That far?"

"You can call your Grandma."

Fields and farms. Silos. Cows, cows, and more cows. No horses around here, JK. Looks like we left horse country behind.

Sylvia babbled on and on nonstop. About the farm not being profitable. Grandma only kept it for her pleasure. Dad said that they could do good business here, like summer camp, horse lessons, or something. But Grandma wouldn't have any of it. Having a farm had always been her dream, a dream she couldn't achieve while Grandfather was working, but when he stopped...

"Can I have your sunglasses?"

Sylvia handed him the glasses and suddenly went all quiet with self-disappointment. She thought, "Why am I such a chatterbox? He's probably wishing he never got involved with me."

"Thanks. That's more like it. This sun is blinding me."

Why has she stopped talking, JK? Timothy wondered as another quiet minute went by. And then he realized that he probably had to entertain 'his date'.

"You want to get behind the wheel?"

"Oh, I don't have my driver's license yet. I won't turn seventeen for another two weeks yet."

"Well, whatever you wish."

Would you ever think she was seventeen, JK? Never.

Sylvia thought, "If he'd really let me drive, maybe, I should give it a try? The road is empty. Or maybe I shouldn't ask now that I've already refused?"

"Whose idea was it to give a Golden Labrador a name like Gypsy King?"

Sylvia startled, surprised at his starting to talk again. She patted Gypsy King's head.

"It was Grandma's. He's named after one of his relatives. Grandma really loved the first Gypsy King. She says he was a great dog."

And she went on and on with stories from the life of Gypsy King's grandparent.

Timothy half-heartedly listened to her chatter.

The car gave a loud snort, though it wasn't clear whether that was the engine.

Sylvia stopped, frightened.

"I checked the car before we hit the road." Timothy was trying to sound calm.

This old junker is beyond any help, JK, whether you fix it or not. It's all worn out. But I'm not trusted to take the Princess out on a motorcycle.

***

The west shore of the lake did turn out to be pretty desolate. Long stretches of white beaches. They found an improvised parking lot, trampled grass, somebody's car parked nearby. They took a steep set of stairs down to the beach. The sand. It was almost snow-white. The deep blue lake. And the waves.

"Too bad, it's windy, so badminton's out. But I brought a ball!"

Timothy went back to the car to bring everything else she had brought along. Sylvia and Gypsy King were running along the shore. Sylvia went and got out a blanket.

Timothy quickly pulled off his shirt, but Sylvia hesitated. What a dumb bathing suit she had. And she was so skinny. Melinda always said that her shoulder blades stuck out like a pair of wings. She probably wasn't kidding either. Anyway. She should have thought before she agreed to go to the beach how uncomfortable it might be to get undressed. Sylvia decisively took off her clothes, trying not to look at Timothy.

"Do you want some sunblock?" She offered him two bottles.

He shook his head no.

"You'll get sunburn."

He took the bottle.

It was a little tricky putting sun block on her own back. But asking him to help? Not in her lifetime. If only Melissa was in her place right now... she would have had guys lined up to help her.

"Should I put some on you too? Maybe, on the nose?" Sylvia was laughingly trying to push away the ever-curious Gypsy King.

Timothy threw a stick into the air and Gypsy King happily took off after it.

"Nice breed," Timothy said admiring the dog.

"Oh yes! He could have easily been a show dog. But Grandma's too lazy to give it any more time. First Gypsy King was a medal winner!"

"Medals? For his breed? Oh, he must have also been a Golden Lab!" Timothy realized. "So, how come he was named Gypsy King?"

"It was his personality. He was always running off somewhere, coming back whenever he pleased. He did at first have some other name, but it didn't stick. It's probably in his official papers. Grandma still has them."

"I see. Why is your chestnut-colored horse named Snowflake, then?"

"After I named the cat Bird, Grandma wouldn't let me give any more names. Since Melinda was sick, she got the task, so she could do something fun. To spite me, we were fighting at the time, she came up with the most unsuitable name she could think of. What she didn't know was that Snowflake had a white spot on her. A really tiny one. And I loved the name! Snowflake!"

"I know. It's under her left kneecap. It's nearly unnoticeable. I couldn't believe my eyes at first."

"Just don't tell anyone. It's my little secret."

"Fine. Then why did you name the cat Bird?"

Sylvia gave out a long sigh, but she went on with the story. "It was our cat's first litter. And she went nuts. She took the kittens one by one and threw them into the outhouse - they all drowned, except for the last one. I took him away. Still, she refused to nurse him. So I had to bottle-feed him myself. He was so funny-looking. Super-small. He looked like a tiny pile of poop when he was sleeping. So I would call him that playfully. And he started answering to it! When Grandma found out, she was upset. We tried every name that rhymed. But the only other name Poop would answer to was Bird."

"I was ten years old." She added apologetically.

Timothy was leaning back on the blanket, looking at her and smiling.

"You know, it didn't surprise me one bit that all your names started with letter M. Melissa, Melinda, Melanie, Mark, Martin and Michael."

How do you like that, JK?

Sylvia's jaw dropped, "You're right! And I've never even noticed."

It was his turn to be surprised, "Seriously? Then, you must not know why out of a sudden your name is Sylvia?"

"Ugh." She sounded very emotional. "I hate my name. It's so stupid. Everyone's name is way better. I'll change it as soon as I'm old enough."

"What do you mean?" He seemed genuinely surprised by her reaction. "It's a very horse-worthy name. It's great!"

Sylvia laughed so hard she nearly cried. Though she did like the fact that he could say something so silly.

"Fine. You made me feel better. I'll keep it. But please promise me you won't pay compliments like that to anyone ever again. Melissa would definitely not like it."

And she started chanting, "Sylvia is a great little horsy!"

Timothy was a little embarrassed by the name word play. He threw Gypsy King's stick and tried to change the subject, "Once, JK and I spent the night with the gypsies."

Sylvia was intrigued, "Tell me more! I've never even seen real gypsies."

"Their troop was moving through the town. They set up camp on the outskirts in the fields. JK's aunt wouldn't let us go check them out, so he came up with the idea to go at night. We couldn't miss the chance to see them before they left. But JK had to be woken up. He's such a sleepyhead. We left town in the middle of the night, but we had no idea where to look for them. We wandered around for almost two whole hours until we spotted a fire. Good thing the gypsies were still up. Or, maybe they never sleep at night. We hung out till the morning, and it was time for them to leave. It was then that JK fell in love with the horses. So did I."

Timothy chuckled.

"These gypsies were so dirty, but you should have seen how well their horses were taken care of. Each had its own bucket for drinking water and the buckets were sparkling clean."

"Weren't you scared of the night? And of the gypsies? What were they like? How could you never have seen horses? Who is this JK? Did you get in a lot of trouble?"

"Of course we did. JK is my cousin. My mother's sister's son. But he was more like a brother to me. I can't even remember myself without him. Where's Timothy? Over with JK. Where's JK? Over with Timothy."

Timothy didn't know why he was telling her all that, but it was pouring out. Sylvia wondered at his strange facial expression.

"So your full name is Timothy?"

He nodded. Sylvia wondered if anyone ever called him by the short version of the name at home, since he didn't seem to like being called Tim much.

"Jay-Kay - what a strange name."

"Well." Suddenly Timothy didn't feel like talking anymore. "These are just the initials. Eventually they turned into a nickname."

"Weren't you scared?"

"We were about ten years old. And there were two of us."

"Once Vince and I went out at night. We were about ten years old, too. We went to the cemetery. That was all my idea."

Who would doubt that, right, JK?

"I can't remember what we were looking for. We almost got there. You know, when you're really scared but trying not to let it show, it turns out okay. All of a sudden, Vince panicked and I got even more frightened because he panicked. And he got more frightened because I got more frightened. And then I got even more frightened! We started hollering and ran home. Woke Grandma. We were in real trouble then too."

"Who is Vince? Another one of Grandma's grandkids?" Timothy smiled.

"No. He's just a friend. Our neighbor."

"A childhood friend?"

"A summer friend. Grandma called us that. It's because we meet only during summers. He's supposed to arrive here soon." Sylvia quietly sighed. "I wonder if he has changed a whole lot."

They got quiet, each thinking of and missing their respective childhood friends. Sylvia, however, couldn't stay still too long. Up she jumped and raised her arms, "Can you do this?"

She went on to perform a cartwheel.

Gypsy King started jumping happily around her. Timothy got up, kicked up the sand with his foot, found a stretch of wet sand near the water, went into a hand stand and proceeded to walk on his hands.

"And can you do this?"

He fell down nearly crushing Gypsy King who was whirling around next to him.

Sylvia tried, her hands sunk into the sand and she collapsed.

"Come over here, it's easier to do on the wet sand."

She did a hand stand and tried to take a 'step'. Timothy grabbed her ankles so she wouldn't fall down.

"Straighten out your back."

She succeeded with a couple of 'steps' on her own. She may have done more had it not been for Gypsy King always getting in the way.

***

Sylvia was zealously digging in the sand. Right next to her Gypsy King was copying her efforts, except he was doing much better.

"Lie down!" She ordered Timothy.

"Now what?" he asked as he was lying down.

"Here's what!"

She quickly started covering him up with sand and patted the mound with great satisfaction. Gypsy King came up looking surprised and sniffed at Timothy's face. The poor guy tried in vain to turn away, but when Gypsy King licked him, he couldn't take it, he got out of the sand and playfully knocked the dog down, "Your turn, shaggy!"

Then, it was Sylvia's turn. Looking at her he started thinking, *Maybe this isn't a bad idea for Grandma, huh, JK? We could bring some sand from here and let 'troublemakers' dig each other in. It'll give everyone five minutes of quiet.*

Sylvia giggled, "Ouch, Gypsy King!"

Timothy turned around. Gypsy King was biting her big toes which were sticking out of the pile of sand.

After that, they sent sailing a large chunk of wood that the waves brought to the shore.

Sylvia thought, "These wild beaches are great except for one thing. What should I do? How easy for the guys. They step aside and they're done. Oh, how it sucks to be a woman." She hesitated for a moment and went into the water.

"You're out of your mind!" Timothy shook his head watching as shivering Sylvia was getting out of the water.

"It's warmer than it looks. And it's so deep. Over on Wasaga Beach the water is probably warmer, but it's only knee-deep, and it's full of people."

"So why do we have all these bags? Should we eat something?"

Timothy tried to light a small fire. But the wind was determined to put it out.

"Here, let me show you. Voila!" And Sylvia got the fire going.

"Wow!" He put out the fire and tried to do what she just did, succeeding only on the third try.

They were roasting marshmallows for dessert.

JK, she brought enough junk to feed the entire African continent. It must be a habit from dealing with the 'troublemakers' on a daily basis.

After lunch, they lay down on a blanket. Gypsy King took the spot in the middle. The sun was no longer scorching, the wind died down. Sylvia once again got that unsettled feeling, she was afraid to look Timothy's way. Gypsy King got up, shook off the sand and went about his gypsy business. Timothy took her hand into his. Sylvia's heart stopped for a moment. She got brave enough to glance his way. He was laying down looking at the sky. Gypsy King returned and stuck his cold nose into the palm of his hand. Timothy sat up and with a look of surprise stared at the girl, the dog, the lake, as though he had just woken up and wondered where he was.

"I didn't know there were gypsies in Canada."

Timothy gave Sylvia a puzzled look. Then he remembered what she was talking about.

"It was back in Europe. We were staying with JK's relatives. They still live there."

"My parents are in Florida right now. I decided not to go with them and come to Grandma's instead."

Easy to figure who's to blame for that, JK. A prince named Vince. Timothy hid his grin.

"Florida was tempting, of course. But going with the parents is like being on a leash. I'll have another chance. I'll go with someone special. Just the two of us..." Sylvia said dreamily. "So how did you communicate with them?"

"With whom?"

"The gypsies."

"Oh! JK. He's real multilingual; the languages just come easy to him. He didn't know the language the gypsies spoke, but they found a way to communicate."

"He sounds like a trooper."

"Yeah, he was."

"Isn't it great here?"

"It's alright."

"What, have you been to a better place?"

"Yeah, I have. Palm trees, beaches full of suntanned girls."

"Well, you've just been everywhere, haven't you?"

"Nah, you can count all that as a dream. Europe. Everything. Everything but JK," he suddenly snapped.

She didn't know what was with him, but looked at him sympathetically.

"Sean says you scream in your sleep."

She stopped, afraid she had said too much. Now he was going to think that she grilled Sean about him - though that was exactly how it was - and would think God knows what else.

"It's still great here! What a blessing it is to live in this world! Everything is just wonderful!" She jumped up and spun around.

He continued sitting with his head down.

"What's the matter?"

"Nothing. Don't worry about it. Sometimes this world has its share of troubles." He sighed.

She knelt next to him, "Maybe I can do something to help you? What if I could? Or what if Grandma could help? Don't worry, she is so kind and helps so many people"

"No." He sounded firm. "It's okay. It's nothing. Just bad dreams."

Sylvia thought, "I bet it has to do with money. My parent's troubles always have to do with money. Our farm is the wrong place to make any money though. I bet Timothy came here for the horses."

"Well, shall we get going?"

"Hold on, I'll be right back." Timothy headed for the shrubs.

Sylvia grabbed the stick away from Gypsy King and was teasing him with it. Timothy returned.

Just like that. He went, he came back. Three hours on the road. I could, of course, ask him to stop at a gas station. No, no way. Sylvia took a deep breath and went over to the shrubs herself. Timothy didn't pay her any attention. She glanced back, he was shaking out the blanket with his back to her.

She was thinking, "It's not a big deal. Or is it? Why am I always so shy about these things? It's such a simple thing - just say "I have to go." No, not with a guy. I wonder if it'll be the same with Vince."

       ***

Having babbled on and on for a while, Sylvia started nodding off. Soon, she was fast asleep. Timothy thought about waking her, but decided he didn't feel like it. Instead, he went deep into his own thoughts.

Timothy shut off the engine.

"Are we here already?" Sylvia woke up and stretched out with a big yawn on her face.

She let Gypsy King out of the truck, while Timothy carried the bags to the door. He pulled a broken watch out of his pocket.

I was going to get a new one in the city, JK. I really was. Well, so much for that, huh. But it was a pretty cool road trip, right?

As he turned around, his eyes met Sylvia's and he smiled.

"We still have fifteen minutes to spare before it's eleven o'clock."

She paused, trying to figure out the meaning of his words and finally smiled back at him.

"Thank you. I had a great time."

"No, thank you." And he offered. "There's a lighthouse marked on the map. It's just south of the place we went today. Would you like to go there some time?"

"Alright."

Sleepily, she rocked back on her feet and then stepped forward right into his arms. He saw her eyes so close, as though she was reaching for him, he bent down to kiss her cheek - but the kiss landed right on the corner of her mouth.

Her eyes opened wide and first words out of her mouth were:

"Mmm... Delicious!"

Timothy looked amused.

I have no idea what I'm doing, how about you, JK? Hmm. Delicious she said.

And off he went to park the pickup.

She thought , "Was it just a dream or did it really happen? Did he really kiss me? Was I supposed to kiss him back?"

"Oh, Grandma! You're still awake?"

"Do you want some dinner?"

"No, thanks."

"How was the trip?"

"It was great!"

Sylvia squeezed her Grandma into a big hug and whispered into her ear. "He kissed me, Grandma! Can you believe it? Do you think he really meant to kiss me?"

"Of course he meant to kiss you, why else would he kiss you then? Oh, my Princess. Just please be sure not to fall head over heels. He's not worth it. He's not even that cute! Snub nose, small eyes..." Grandma was using the old tried and true family trick that was used on her back in the day as well. And it even worked on her for a while, until she met Grandpa that is.

"Grandma! What are you doing trying to ruin my first kiss, huh? And I'll have you know - his eyes are perfectly normal!"

Back in her own room Sylvia thought about the kiss again. She stared at her reflection in the mirror. She looked nothing like she wished she would look. Her nose was red with sunburn, her cheek... well, it probably would have been better not to look into the mirror at all. Good thing it was just her right cheek. At least Timothy didn't have to stare at it the entire time of their drive in the car. Her hair was a total mess too, and full of sand. She was quite the looker. So why did he kiss her then? Maybe, there was something special about her that attracted him after all? Or, maybe he kissed her just because it was the thing to do? Everybody kissed at the end of a date. Now really upset with herself, Sylvia turned away from the mirror.

Timothy, totally beat after the six-hour drive, finally had the chance to stretch out his limbs in his own bed. The road was flashing behind his closed eyes, and then more and more road, fields stretching all the way out to the horizon. Corn. Farmhouses, few and far in between. Timothy sank into a deep slumber and this time he didn't dream any dreams.

**

Suddenly Sylvia didn't feel like sharing any details of her trip with her cousins.
"It was fine." She shrugged them off at breakfast.
The 'girls' looked quite puzzled. Grandma suspiciously fixed her eyes on her youngest granddaughter.
After breakfast, Sylvia stopped at the stables.
"Hey!"
"Hey!" Timothy briefly glanced her way and went on working.
"My nose got totally burnt." Sylvia reported immediately growing irritated with herself.
She thought, "Why couldn't I come up with anything clever to say?!"
"Yeah. I think my shoulders did too."
He turned to face her.
"How's that cheek?"
"Same old."
"Another two-three years and you'll forget all about it."
When he got up to look again, she was already out of sight.
I must have said something stupid, JK.
Timothy went back to his work.
In the afternoon, Sean handed him a tube of skin cream.
For sunburned shoulders, JK, can you believe her?
"So where's Princess herself?"
"Gone. She and Melissa took the 'troublemakers' out to visit some friends. They'll be gone the entire day!" Sean couldn't have sounded more excited.

"Boy, I am not crazy about all this." Grandma sounded worried.
"About what?" Grandpa was surprised.
"About this Tim Miller character."
"I thought you were happy with his work. Remember, you even mentioned that we should give him a pay raise!"
"I'm talking about our Princess." Grandma let out a deep sigh. "She might just be silly enough to decide that this could be serious."
"So what? She'll be seventeen in two weeks. Remember, when we met? Had you even turned sixteen then?"

"But I was so mature and independent. This new generation is so slow to mature."

Grandpa smiled, remembering the young independent Grandma. The truth was he never got to forget her young ways, because she hasn't changed a bit since then. Did all these years really pass since the day they first met? He could hardly believe it.

"We should run a check on him." Grandma sounded determined.

"You're free to do as you wish, but I would stay out of it - let them figure everything out on their own. Otherwise, you'll stir up trouble. You know how it goes with a forbidden fruit." And he remembered everything as though it was yesterday.

"I wish Vince would get here already. The last thing we need is this Miller fellow." Grandma now laughed. "Did you see he's got a button for a nose! Can you imagine us with button-nosed great-grandkids? How would I even rock those buttons to sleep?" Grandma held out her arms as though she was cradling a baby. "No button noses for us!"

Grandpa held her to his chest and gave her a kiss.

They heard loud footsteps. The 'troublemakers' who must have returned from their visit, peeked their heads in and went on trampling through the house.

"I'd better go get some dinner warmed up." Grandma sighed.

"You should have seen them! Grandpa and Grams! They were totally making out! Just like Melissa and Eric do!" The 'troublemakers' couldn't contain themselves.

"Eww! No way!" Melissa was shocked. "They're too old for that!"

"Luck doesn't seem to be on your side today." Jack burst into laughter. He was Vince's great-uncle, but Vince always called him uncle. Uncle Jack. It was their thing.

Grandma laid her cards to the side and took a deep breath. They were sitting around Jack's living room playing poker, a small and tight bunch of good old friends.

"More beer?" Jack offered. "Come on. Come give me a hand in the kitchen."

"Alright. What is it? Let it all out." He asked once he and Grandma were back in the kitchen.

"I wish Vince would get here soon, Jack. I'm worried - our Princess, it seems, is quite taken with this Tim Miller. And what do I know about him? He answered my ad in the paper. He had a couple of average recommendations. He's not one of us. I know he's quite the worker, one in a million - but something seems off. Something just doesn't add up."

"Where is he from?"

"Small town, middle of nowhere, in British Columbia. I did, however, happen to grab a copy of his contract and a letter of recommendation on my way here."

"You 'happened' to bring them, huh?" Jack teased. "Well, let's see them. I've got an old friend who works out that way. I'll call and see if he's got anything on this guy."

"I wouldn't be surprised if he doesn't. The guy's so quiet. I wish I knew what he was really like. What kind of family he's from. Just in case."

"Alright. I'll do everything I can."

Suddenly, Grandma's luck in cards returned.

***

"Well, he lives with his mother. His parents are divorced. High-school dropout. Does a fair share of job-hopping, never stays in one place too long. Traveled a lot since the age of fifteen, but his criminal record is clean. Just a driver's license lost and reinstated, but that's all."

"Wow, you must have special agents working for you on the other end of the country!" Grandpa just started feeling impressed as he realized, "Jack! You've got old friend Jack wrapped around your little finger again, and he would move mountains for you if he had to!"

"Quit with your jealousy!" Grandma smiled and then became serious "I just don't like this. The guy's almost twenty-two and he still hasn't figured out what he wants in this life. He's just floating about."

"Well, what do you expect him being raised without a father?"

"How can we get our Princess to open her eyes and to see that he's nothing more than a pair of hot pants? You know what first love can be like. Especially for a girl like her. It could be such a tragedy - the wrong kind of guy, the wrong kind of life. I'll just die if my baby girl ends up suffering or unhappy. And for whom?"

"You're being way too overprotective. Let them figure everything out on their own. It'll be alright. And in any case, you shouldn't worry because our Princess takes exactly after her Grandma."

"I'm going to have a talk with him."

"I wouldn't."

***

"Tim, I need to talk to you."

"Me?"

Grandma hesitated unsure where to start. Timothy continued looking at her in perfect calmness, a little intrigued if anything.

"I ran a background check on you."

"So?"

"Well, it wasn't too reassuring. You're constantly job-hopping. Dropped out of high school."

He shrugged:

"So what?"

The way he talked really got to Grandma. He was an introvert, quiet, keeping to himself, polite enough, but had this overwhelmingly aloof attitude. Don't bother me, don't pry me out of my shell. He was just different.

"Do you want to know why I resorted to doing this? I'm worried sick about Sylvia. She's not like Melissa or Melinda, though those two could also use a watchful eye. Still, I know all of their boyfriends. Sylvia's still just a kid - so good-hearted and trusting - she's been that way since she was born. And we love her for it. But you're... you've obviously been around the block a few times. I don't want you to take advantage of her for the sake of some summer fun. Is this what you really want? ("Oh boy, I'm getting carried away.") I'm not against you going on a few road trips together, but please, well, control your urges. I won't have you give her any cause for tears. Don't take all this personally, but consider yourself warned."

Grandma stopped, feeling disappointed with her speech. Timothy, puzzled, waited for more, but nothing else came, so he nodded, turned around and left.

She should really consider getting a new filing cabinet if she's going to keep doing background checks every time a granddaughter goes on a date. With four granddaughters and a bunch of guys following them around, Melissa's dates alone would take up several drawers. Right, JK? Who was taking advantage, huh, JK? Did you see any advantage taking place? That was something. So close.

Sylvia snuck out from around the corner, grabbed his arm and whispered:

"What did Grandma want from you?"

"I don't know!"

"It had to do with me, didn't it?!"

Timothy shrugged.

It was just a lecture. About having protected sex. Or maybe about not having any sex? What did she want from me, JK?

"That is so humiliating! On the other hand, it could be kind of funny Grandma being so overprotective, right?"

"It's no big deal. Let's go. I'll get Snowflake saddled up for you."

"Let's! If I don't get away now, I might get stuck with the 'troublemakers' again. They drove me absolutely batty when we were visiting friends. The friend's kids came down with something, chicken pox I think. It was like a hospital over there. But it was a birthday, so they expected to be entertained. Melissa ditched me and drove off to Eric's, so I had to fend for myself."

Sylvia rode off in a much better mood.

Later Timothy went to meet her and to take her horse.

Oh, JK, just look how awkward she is in a saddle. Like a dog on a fence. Timothy frowned and only then noticed that Sylvia was clutching something in her hands.

A guy he'd never seen before beat him to her.

"Vince! You're here!" Sylvia was absolutely beside herself with glee, though of course she had promised herself time and time again to keep her cool when they finally met.

"Let me introduce you two." Sylvia offered as she was passing Snowflake into Timothy's hands. "This is Vince, my good old friend!" She glanced at him with such joy. "Timothy, also my friend, he's our new stableman."

"Just a worker in the stables." Timothy corrected her.

Vince nodded but didn't shake hands, just glanced over Timothy. Timothy didn't want to seem over-eager, so he went about his business.

As he turned to take one more look at them, he heard Vince's voice. "I brought you a little something. Do you want it now or should I tease you a little till your birthday?"

"Do you want my curiosity to totally kill me? Give it to me this minute! Oh, wait!" Sylvia suddenly turned away and took off after Timothy handing him a baseball cap full of tiny wild strawberries. "I picked these for you. I found quite a spot in the woods. I'll show you later."

She ran away. Timothy threw a few berries into his mouth.

Later that night a beaming Sylvia showed up at the stables. She saw her baseball cap on one of the boxes still half full with tiny strawberries.

"I left some for you."

"Aw, thanks! I didn't even get to try any."

They sat next to one another and ate the strawberries in complete silence.

They sat out too long. The taste was way better in the morning, JK.

"Vince brought me a kite for a gift. It's huge!" Sylvia boasted. It was strange, but now that Vince was here, she found it so much easier to talk to Timothy. Or maybe she just got used to him and stopped feeling so shy?

"He says it took him a while to figure out what to give me and this is the best he could do." She laughed. "I'm going to try flying it tomorrow."

"Together with Vince?"

The 'troublemakers' will be beyond themselves, JK. It's going to be crazy.

"No, just me. Vince is going golfing tomorrow. Are you kidding, he's all mature and grown-up now, I can hardly see him flying a kite. I bet he'll be back to his old self by the end of summer." Sylvia puffed out her cheeks imitating the grow-up Vince and ran off holding the empty strawberry-stained baseball cap.

Timothy shook his head.

I bet you one week, JK. She'll have him flying the kite in one week's time. And by the end of the summer she'll be playing golf.

The kite wasn't taking off. The 'troublemakers' were loud in their indignation. They tried a bike. It didn't help. The kite kept falling down. Timothy could no longer take it.

Seems like a normal kite for all I know, JK. How did you and I grow up with no kites?

"Why don't you bring some old kite, one that flies well." Timothy asked Martin. He was wrong to think Martin would go at it alone. The 'troublemakers' never did anything alone. All three of them took off arguing on the way what kite they thought was best and who was going to carry it.

Timothy compared the build of the two kites.

What's the trick here, JK?

He took out his pocket knife and questioningly looked at Sylvia.

"Do it." She nodded.

He shortened the planks. Not it. He changed the angle. The kite flew! Timothy put away the knife and went back to the horses not even bothering to look back.

***

"Grandma, what's the matter with Vince? At first, he's all mine and now I can hardly get him to notice me. It's like I don't exist! What am I supposed to do, pull on his sleeve?"

Grandma didn't get to answer. Melissa laughed, "He's teasing you. Don't even think about the sleeve-pulling. You should pretend he doesn't exist for you either. Pretty soon he'll be back begging, I promise."

"Does it have to be this complicated?"

Melissa laughed till she had tears in her eyes. "If you want uncomplicated, you've got Tim Miller. He is totally uncomplicated and square."

"What are you talking about! Don't you dare say that about him!" Sylvia ambushed Melissa and threw her on the couch.

Grandma jumped to pull them apart. And there she thought that their cat-fights were a thing of the past; she thought she just had the 'troublemakers' to get through and peace and quiet would be back in her house.

At dinner Vince was talking about a musician coming into town. He'd heard this guy once before in Toronto. It was the chance of a lifetime that this saxophone player would be playing live right here in one of the local pubs. Melissa noted that she couldn't stand listening to musicians in the pub, there was always too much smoke and too much noise with the musician trying to play over the crowd. There was no fun in that so she wasn't going. He said he would go with the McGregors. To miss such an opportunity? Never in his lifetime!

Sylvia was expecting Vince to ask her to come along, but he didn't. She didn't know if it was him teasing her again or him not even realizing what her expectations might have been. He kept making jokes remembering yesterday's party. "I wish he wouldn't talk about that!" Sylvia thought. But he still wasn't asking her to come with him. She got up, snuck out the door and ran straight into Timothy.

"Are you going to check out that saxophone player on Friday?"

"Yeah, I was thinking about it. What about you?"

She didn't say anything. It wasn't like she could complain about Vince to him anyway. She shrugged her shoulders. Grandma has already wondered where her Princess got that shoulder-shrugging habit.

"Do you want to come with me?"

"It's a deal."

Vince showed up on the porch looking for her.

"So, Princess, are you going to the pub with us on Friday?"

She couldn't believe it. Great timing.

"Timothy already asked me. I'm going with him. Goodnight."

Sylvia thought, "Did I just invite myself? Or, did he really mean to invite me? It seemed if I hadn't asked, he would have never invited me. It does seem like I did invite myself. Oh well. That'll teach Vince a lesson. Especially after what happened yesterday. He treated me like I was a... and all because I let him kiss me." Sylvia was going to keep as far away from him as she could at the bar. She'd be with Timothy anyway. She thought, "How great will that be! Even if I did invite myself. Boy, why was my entire body so itchy?" Sylvia took off her t-shirt and stared at her reflection in the mirror - was she beautiful or not, after all? Ouch, and what was that?!

***

"It seems the Princess has come down with a case of chickenpox." Sean mentioned in the morning. "I'm taking her to the doctor's. You should manage without me just fine."

Timothy nodded in reply.

The case of chickenpox was confirmed. Sylvia got locked away since Grandma couldn't remember which of her grandkids had chickenpox and which didn't and the last thing she needed was a home turned hospital, so maybe they would get lucky.

Late in the evening, as he was headed for his place, Timothy saw a faint light in the second story window.

She's still up, JK. I wonder how she is.

He tried whistling. She didn't hear. He glanced up at the porch roof, took off his shoes so they wouldn't bang on the sheet of metal covering it, and with a couple of lithe moves he was up on the window sill.

Sylvia was sitting on the bed all bundled up in a blanket, looking sad and covered in spots.

"Timothy? Aren't you supposed to be at the bar?"

He shook his head.

"How are you doing?"

"Everything is so itchy. I'm just sitting here trying to keep from scratching but it's like my hands have a mind of their own. You're so crazy to come here, you'll get sick. Grown-ups can get really sick. I've even got a fever and all."

"I've had it already. JK too."

Sylvia stuck out her hand and scratched her head. Timothy sat down next to her, leaned her head to take a look and whistled with surprise. "Wow, you've even got some on your head! Don't scratch it."

"Why not scratch if it's itching?"

"I don't remember why. You're not supposed to. Use your willpower."

"I don't have any." Sylvia felt so sad she could only complain. "I'm feeling so lousy."

Her eyes looked sunken with an unhealthy glow. He touched her forehead and it was really hot.

"Should I go get your Grandma?"

"No, it's okay. The doctor said I'd be this way for a few days."

"You'll be better in no time."

"So what do you think? How come every time I'm planning to do something with you, something totally awful happens to me? Every time I get covered with some disgusting thing, so I can't even look at my own self. I really wanted to go to this stupid bar! Maybe, we would get fifteen extra minutes again and..."

Timothy caught on and laughed.

"Well, if that's the only thing upsetting you..."

JK, she's one of a kind, isn't she?

He kissed her gently touching her lips with his.

"Is this good?"

"Yes." Sylvia mumbled. "With you it feels right. And with Vince it was all wrong. I only wanted to compare and he started... anyway, it was just wrong."

"Alright, why don't you get some sleep and get better. We'll have plenty of chances to go out."

"Tell me about the gypsies." Sylvia sounded sleepy. Just as her hand started reaching for her head, Timothy caught her wrist and Sylvia obediently stuffed it back under the blanket.

"What do you want to hear?"

"Are they just like in the movies?"

"Not quite." Timothy put a pillow against the wall, leaned back and started telling about the time he saw a young gypsy woman dance. "She had this beautiful coin necklace on and it jingled along with her movements."

Remember, JK?

"Her moves were so fascinating, it was like watching fire dance. All her skirts were swirling about her fast legs."

Sylvia closed her eyes. Bright gypsy skirts were swirling like a tornado in front of her. She was falling asleep fast.

Timothy woke to Grandma's loud voice. Quickly, he realized where he was. He reached out, the forehead was now cool. Quickly, he snuck out of the window.
It would be quite a scene had Grandma caught me here, JK.
Immediately, he came face to face with Sean.
"I've been looking for you." Sean said. "Let's go take care of the firewood."
Timothy looked around for his shoes and, barefoot, followed Sean.

***

"Oh, Grandma, if only you knew what kind of dream I had!"
"Here, sweetheart, get some more to drink, the more you drink the sooner you'll get better."
"I am already much better, really."
Sylvia looked out the window to see Gypsy King tear apart a pair of work boots. She laughed out loud. Grandma came up to look, gasped, and with her thundering voice yelled for someone to immediately take the prey away from Gypsy King and return it to the owner. Only Sylvia knew right away who the owner was.

And with Vince it was all wrong. Timothy remembered suddenly. *She was trying to compare, JK. Compare what? How can you compare something like this? Just take it and compare it?*
"Hold up! We're not making splinters here, what's the matter with you?" Sean was yelling.
"No matter!" Timothy flung down the axe.
What is the matter with me, JK? What an idiot she is. She thinks she can compare...
He tried to get a hold of himself.
Why would I care about her anyway, JK?
If he knew how to do anything it was to get a hold of himself. He needed to calm down.

A few days later Sylvia reappeared. "I've been released from prison! Where have you been?"
He kept silent and didn't even turn to her.
"Timothy?"
Not a word.
"Timothy, are you alright?"
"I'm fine. You know what, why don't you get out of here? You've annoyed your Grandma enough, don't you think so? Try it out with Vince one more time, maybe

you'll have more luck. Maybe you should try with every guy in the neighborhood. I'm too busy for this."

He grabbed his buckets and cluttered into the street right past Sylvia, not even bothering to look at her.

Completely stunned by his words, all Sylvia could do was stare after him as he was walking away. It slowly dawned on her what exactly he was talking about. She sunk onto a wooden crate and burst into tears.

There were times she felt that maybe he was right to get so angry, maybe she did ruin something so good, tender and pure only they shared. Other times she thought that he was an idiot completely out of line with no right to say what he did, because she didn't do anything unusual. She always ran her mouth, she should have never told him.

They were not speaking to each other. Grandma was rejoicing on the inside. This way it's much better.

***

"Everyone's got something going on except for Tim. Sylvia, cut it out." Grandma insisted.

"I am not going with him. And in any case, why do I have to go see the doctor? I'm almost all better."

"Just for my reassurance, please. The doctor said it would be good to come see him."

Would you look at her, JK, such an angel. Could fool anyone.

They were driving in complete silence, grumpy and avoiding all eye contact. The ride was very jerky.

Sylvia thought, "I bet he's driving like this on purpose. So let him. I couldn't care less."

Sylvia was back quickly from the doctor. Timothy turned the key in the ignition. The car didn't start. He cursed, got out, popped the hood and stared into it, in deep thought. Sylvia felt bored as she stared out the window while he was trying to fix the car. He was really angry with not being able to start this old junker, even if it was no fault of his own. Suddenly, a bright idea struck him and he crawled under the car to check things out under there.

"Aaaaah!"

Sylvia jumped out and peeked under the old truck. She couldn't help herself and burst out laughing. At the very least, she managed to bite her tongue. This probably wasn't a good time to tease him, he looked pretty miserable as it was. Something that looked to her like a broken muffler was lying on top of him.

Timothy crawled out holding his face with his hands.

"You think your eyes are still intact?"

"I don't know."

"Well, let me see." She pulled away his hands.

"I guess I can still see."

Sylvia called her Grandma. Grandma called the mechanic's shop.

They were sitting at the mechanic's. Timothy was icing his face. The mechanics looked at him from time to time and chuckled. To Timothy's surprise, they said the car would be ready in about three hours.

You think they can really bring it back to life, JK?

"Well, should we keep waiting here?" Sylvia asked.

"For three hours? Let's go for a walk." Timothy threw the ice-pack into the trash and they walked out.

People stared at him. The sales-clerk who sold him the band for his watch *(I finally bought it, JK!)* couldn't help but ask what happened.

"Do I look that handsome?" Timothy touched his swollen face.

Sylvia nodded.

Timothy crinkled his nose, "Let's go back to the shop then."

"I've got an idea! Let's go to the movies. It's always dark there. And there's probably not a soul there this time a day."

"You're a genius!"

Isn't she, JK?

"I just know how you must feel." Sylvia sighed. "There are often times I'd rather stick my head into the sand than to have people look at me or pay any attention to me."

Head into the sand, JK.

***

Timothy bought popcorn and coke for the two of them.

"It's supposed to be a comedy and he's just staring at the screen eyes wide-open, not even smiling. I wonder if he hates it. By the way, he does look pug-nosed from this side," she thought.

"What?" He leaned down.

"Nothing."

"Do you want to leave? Are you bored?"

"No."

What would happen if she didn't agree to get this stupid popcorn and both of them had their hands free, would he hold her hand then?

"I was as close to him as I am to you right now." Timothy said as they were returning from the movies.

Do you remember that, JK?

"Close to whom?"

"The actor playing the bad guy."

"Really?"

"Yeah! JK and I were washing cars one summer. Wiping windshields, that is. At a large intersection. We were trying to make some money that way. The driver hands JK a dollar bill and JK tells him if he knew better he would have brought a notebook for an autograph. The guy laughed, got out a pen and signed right on the dollar bill. It was then that I recognized him as that actor."

Timothy got quiet.

Even though Sylvia didn't expect it, he went on to finish the story. "JK laughed about splitting up that dollar bill. We shared everything, always. So I said we should take turns, first he keeps it, and then I do. So the dollar bill roamed from me to him and back. Everyone was jealous of us."

"And then what?"

"We stopped caring about autographs so much. I don't even remember where that dollar bill ended up, whether I have it or JK."

"That's exactly how Vince and I were. Everything was shared. Except I tried to play smart at times. If I really liked something, I would offer to keep it for a while. He would forget all about it. And that was exactly what I hoped for."

They both laughed.

"Did he come to Canada?"

"Who, JK?"

"No, the actor."

Timothy hesitated a while.

"You know what, let's consider it was all a dream. Alright?" He said finally, his voice sounding strange with irony.

"I was quite the laughingstock. I was always making up stories, fantasizing about a pirate ship, trips to Paris that I went on. So I stopped."

"Making up stories?"

"No, telling them. How do you think it might be when you imagine Paris all the time, its streets, smells and sounds, and then you really do end up there and everything is different than you imagined? Would you be better off not going?"

Timothy had to think for a moment. He had never fantasized in his whole life. *What would it be like, JK, to find yourself in the real world that you had always imagined? Would you be disappointed?*

"Have you ever imagined your farm or this town after you left them differently than they were in reality?"

"A million times!"

"And what did that do?" He was curious.

Surprised, Sylvia wasn't sure what to say. "It's true! Why didn't I think of it myself? My Paris and the real Paris are two different cities and whether they look the same or different doesn't matter. It couldn't hurt anything."

She nodded her head, "That's it. I'm going to Paris. To Barcelona. Rome, Venice. And also, to Australia."

"Sometimes it's quite the opposite of what you say." Timothy said. "When you are not thinking or imagining anything ahead of time, it will be what it is. But then you get to the place and you feel like you've been there, everything is familiar; you even know what's around the corner and... You don't ever want to leave. And whatever happens there only adds to your happiness. You may be the only one who feels that way, nobody else."

Except for you, JK. We always felt each other's feelings.

Sylvia thought, "What place he's talking about, our farm? It couldn't be - the farm is nothing special."

"Where did you feel that way?"

"Well, there are few spots on the globe. You just have to know, don't you?"

That comment made Sylvia sad, so she pouted.

He took her hand, "I'm sorry, I don't feel like talking about it right now, not even to you."

He sounded sorry for his words.

They walked holding hands all the way to the auto-shop.

Sylvia thought, "NOT EVEN TO YOU, he said! My hands broke straight into sweat. I bet he wasn't too crazy about holding a sweaty palm."

Back in the car Sylvia couldn't stop talking. So much had happened while she was sick, and they hadn't been talking. Bird brought a dead baby rat to Grandma. Grandma totally freaked out that they had rats, so she turned the entire house upside-down and was planning to do the same to the barns. The whole thing seemed very strange, though. Bird is too old to kill any rats; he had probably found it already dead. But Grandma didn't even want to hear it. She was on a roll. Grandpa convinced her to rent out a part of their farm land. It's not like they were using it anyway. And somebody had agreed to rent it already, even though it was the beginning of summer. It was too good to be true. Everyone was curious about the future tenants. Her parents sent a card. It came from Florida. Poor Melissa was so bummed out, she was now responsible for the 'troublemakers'. The 'troublemakers' didn't seem to be too excited either.

Timothy stopped the pick-up at the front porch.

"We're home already." Sylvia sounded disappointed.

She looked at his swollen cheek and made a scary face, "Aren't you afraid that you have gotten the curse from me?"

"What curse?" He smiled.

She keeps you on your toes, JK.

"What do you mean what curse? Every time you and I go somewhere together, something nasty happens. First, it was only me. And now it's also you. Maybe, it's your turn to pay."

"Well, I'd rather have it be me than you. I'll get by."

Would you believe it, JK? Talk about coincidence.

"Are you going to get out of there?" Grandma was knocking on the window of the truck. She gasped as she looked inside. "Tim, what happened to your face?"

"A family curse." He smiled.

Sylvia was thinking to herself, "Even when he smiles, his eyes still look sad. Maybe, not sad, but there's just something strange about them."

***

As though incidentally, Grandma would drop comments like: "Seems like a strong enough guy, except the neck's too thin." "Look at him eat, he gulps everything down without chewing, no different from Gypsy King." "Does he ever wash his hands?" And other comments of the same sort.

It was weird. When Grandma mocked Timothy, Sylvia couldn't see any humor in it. The comments were true, just like everything else Grandma always said. It was just that she had a special talent of going for the weakest spot and exposing it to everyone around.

His neck really was thin. Though he was always so calm, strong and self-assured, the neck somehow made him seem endearingly vulnerable. And of course, he gulped. He was always late for dinner and always in a hurry to leave. And his hands might just be permanently stained.

Timothy was putting an old abandoned barn into order and in it he found a swing. A steady wooden plank was attached to the still durable old chains. Sylvia couldn't help but come and check out all the noise Timothy was making back at the barn.

"Oh, that's the old swing Vince and I used to have when we were little. What are you going to do with it?"

"I'll fix it up for the 'troublemakers'. They are too old for the tire swing anyway. Where did this swing used to be?"

"It was on the same tree the tire swing is on. Same spot even."

"On the tree?" Timothy sounded surprised.

Sylvia didn't see what the big deal was, just wrap the chains around the branch and find a way to fasten them.

"Do you know anybody who can weld around here?"

As it turned out, Sylvia did know a welder.

"You want to come along?"

Of course! She had sensed an adventure and absolutely had to get involved. Except, she wasn't quite sure of what he had in mind.

Grandma gave a go-ahead for fixing up the swing without asking too much of Tim's plans. Little did she know this would involve riding a motorcycle around the whole county and presenting her with additional expenses, albeit very modest.

The new swing was delivered on the pick-up and looked very solid. Two V-shaped metal bases had a beam bolted to them. The beam held two rings with two metal pipes welded to them. The wooden plank was attached between the two pipes.

Timothy was busy with the cement.

"So what happened to all the chains?" Sylvia was surprised.

It seemed that the only part used from the old swing was the wooden plank and Sylvia wasn't even sure it was the same one.

"I traded them in. For these pipes." Timothy shrugged.

"The last things I need are scraps of metal all over the yard." Grandma grumbled. "You kids would do anything to avoid real work. Is this even safe?"

"I'll be the first one to try." Timothy promised, trying to keep Gypsy King away from the swing. It was too late. A large paw print was forever to remain in the cemented base of the swing.

The 'troublemakers' were squealing with excitement and fighting over whose turn it was on the swing. As Sylvia was looking at them, all she could do was envy them. Back in her days of the old swing chained to the tree, you could never swing that high.

When the 'troublemakers' left for a play-date, Sylvia came up to the swing. She grabbed the pipe with her hand and jumped up onto the wooden plank.

Higher. Higher. She was practically perpendicular to the ground. Then she grew tired and stopped pumping her legs. The swing slowly came to a stop. Sylvia jumped off.

"What do you think?" Timothy was approaching.

"Awesome! Did you see? Did you see how high you can go? I wonder if you can do a full 360 on these."

"You can."

"You sure?"

"Let's go!"

They stood across from each other holding onto the pipes and started taking turns at pumping the swing. It was easier and faster when the two of them did it. They flew higher and higher, reaching and stopping at the vertical point, but it wasn't quite enough to do a complete turn. The feeling of being upside-down for that split second waiting to flip over was unbelievable. But they couldn't quite flip yet.

Finally, Timothy gave it his all and with a powerful push the swing stilled vertically in the air for a second and flipped all the way over. Timothy stopped pumping and hung on the pipes trying to slow the swing down.

Sylvia jumped off. Her eyes burnt with excitement. And then, she saw Grandma. Poor Grandma was standing next to the swing, her hand on her chest, her lips trembling.

"What if Sylvia fell and hurt herself?" She screamed at Timothy.

"Grandma! I know what I'm doing!"

"You think so? I want this swing out of here come nighttime!"

"Why?" Timothy shrugged.

"How dare you ask! You two are supposedly grown-up and still dumb enough to do something like that, let alone the 'troublemakers'. What if they decide to try it?"

"They didn't see us do it and they won't come up with this on their own. Even if they did, they won't have enough strength. And if they do, then they won't fall off."

He suddenly felt embarrassed and looked away, "It's what I think anyway."

"Don't take it apart until the 'troublemakers' are back." Sylvia whispered as she was leaving.

She knew her family well. The grandsons wailed so loudly trying to get Grandma to leave the swing that the latter gave in after she made Sylvia swear not to do any such tricks ever again.

"I can understand our Princess, she can be a bit of an airhead at times, but you're almost twenty-two, it's about time you knew better." Grandma was grumbling, but she no longer sounded angry.

Timothy didn't say anything.

The storm's over, JK. If I'd known this would happen, I wouldn't have gotten involved.

    ***

Late that evening Timothy was sitting on the dock looking over the river. He rolled up his pants, and the water felt nice and cool against his feet.

"Can I sit with you?"

Timothy moved over making room for her. Sylvia wasn't starting the conversation.

What's the matter with her, JK? So quiet.

"Why are you sad?"

"No biggie. It's just that I had that chicken pox right on my birthday. It was the first boring birthday I ever had."

"And I don't even have a gift for you." Timothy sounded disappointed.

Of course, she had her birthday, JK. Seventeen.

"Let's consider the swing a present. Nothing could top that!" Sylvia reassured him.

"Well, it was meant for the troublemakers. But I'm glad you like it."

"You bet I do!" Sylvia exclaimed and then after a moment of silence she added, "Don't be mad at Grandma."

"I'm not. It's no joke to be responsible for seven grandkids all at once." He smiled.

"Does it remind you of your childhood? I mean you built them a hut, a swing, and fixed their tree house."

"No, I envy them. JK and I, we never had a summer like this, except for that one time in Europe."

"You didn't build huts? How could you even survive without them?"

"Not too well." He laughed and went on explaining. "Where could we build it in a city of millions? We did have a swing. At the park. JK and I 'orbited the Moon' on it regularly, like you and I did today. We did it together or took turns. The cool thing to do was not the flip but to jump off at the highest point, before the swing came to a stop. Don't even think of trying it. Or your Grand..."

"Sylvia!" Grandma yelled loudly from the porch.

Unwillingly, Sylvia stood up. So did Timothy.

"Good night." And she was off.

The next night, as though by some magnetic power, Sylvia was drawn to the river. Timothy was already sitting on the dock, and there was no need to ask him to move - he had already made a spot for her to sit.

How could he know that she would show up? Was it a coincidence? Or, could it be that he was hoping she would come?

"What's the matter? I can tell something is wrong. You can talk to me."

"I will, some day. I need some time. To deal. On my own."

Oh JK.

Grandma came out to the porch. She was about to call for Sylvia but then stopped. "Here they are," she thought, "sitting in plain sight as though on the palm of a hand. How would I like it being called home like a little girl when I'm talking to a young man? I'll give it another half hour."

A sleepy Sylvia was home on her own in just twenty minutes.

The next night Timothy waited again, but in vain. The lights were on all over the house, he could hear excited voices.

I guess no company tonight, huh, JK? He went home to sleep.

"I waited for you last night."

"I know. I saw. You know how badly I wanted to get out of there? I kept thinking we would be about done."

"What were you guys doing?"

"We were baking pies, cookies and a big pie. The McGregors are having a party tomorrow; their Grandmother is seventy, so it's a milestone. It's not a party without Grandma's pies." Sylvia laughed.

"So you won't be here tomorrow either." Timothy's sigh was barely audible.

What, was he disappointed? Disappointed not to get to see her?

"I would love to, but won't be back till well after midnight."

And, defying all her expectations, he suddenly said. "I'll still be waiting for you after you get back."

Sylvia was the only one not up for going at all. Everyone else was so excited about the party. But she wouldn't say a word about not going. Grandma wouldn't have any of that. No way.

After the party, as soon as the tires squeaked into the yard, Sylvia flew out of the car and ran towards the river. "He's probably gone by now. It's too late."

"I want you in the house in ten minutes!" Grandma yelled after her.

A dark figure stood up in the twilight to greet her. Sylvia thought with joy, "He's waiting!"

She was running so fast, she nearly knocked him into the dark water. He grabbed onto her, so he wouldn't fall in. Sylvia grabbed onto him. She leaned into him and he kissed her. They stood silent for a moment. Timothy was the first to speak, "Go. Or they'll cook you up alive. See you tomorrow."

"It's today." She laughed and ran off.

"What do you think you're doing?!" Grandma confronted her. "You'll be fine sleeping in till noon, but don't forget that your little boyfriend has to get up at the crack of dawn. What, a whole day is not enough for you two?"

"I'll get up early too." Sylvia promised.

Grandma headed to her room, grumbling unhappily about what could be so good about hanging out on the dock so late at night.

Sylvia thought with wonder, "Grandma doesn't get it. No way to cuddle up to her and tell her everything. How could it be this way with my own beloved Grandma? Why did I feel I had to choose between Timothy and Grandma? Why couldn't Grandma treat him like one of our own? The way she'd always treated all our friends?"

Sylvia was tossing and couldn't fall asleep, envisioning Timothy kissing her over and over again. Here she was, running, pushing into him. He was kissing her. Again, she was running, pushing. He was kissing her.

***

"What is it you and Tim talk about every night?" Melinda inquired at the breakfast table.

Sylvia shrugged her shoulders. She wasn't sure. What did they talk about?

"About the things we did when we were little. About Vince and JK."

"About Vince!" Melissa burst out laughing till she choked and started coughing.

She wiped the tears from her eyes and continued. "So what do you say about Vince?"

"I told about the time we were building the hut. We had two designs and weren't sure which was better to go with. So Vince built both. You've got to remember them; they were around for a long while."

"That's so kindergarten." Melissa shook her head.

"And what is it you and Eric talk about?" Melanie inquired.

And Melinda added in a mean and loud voice. "Do you really think it's talking that they do?"

The appearance of Grandma with cups in her hands was the only thing that prevented a bloody massacre.

She felt she could do whatever she pleased with him! He was totally under her spell. If she told him to jump into the river, he would. Without even asking why. This feeling of ownership and power was deeply satisfying to her. Suddenly, Sylvia knew exactly how Melissa must feel. Except Sylvia didn't need anyone but Timothy. No other admirers were necessary. Only him. And she didn't really need him to jump into the water for her. But once in a while she still tried how much power her charm had on him.

"Am I beautiful?"

"Yes."

"Very beautiful?"

"Very."

"The most beautiful around?"

"Yes."

"Yeah right. Maybe, I should try out for a model?"

"If you want." He smiled.

She's a piece of work, JK.

"Only if you made it into the jury." Sylvia laughed and went on with the interrogation, "So who's more beautiful, Melissa or I?"

He looked at her. "You are."

"Me or Snowflake?" Sylvia was goofing around.

"Don't be silly. I can't compare you. You are two completely different kinds of horses."

They both laughed.

"Do you like me?"

"Yes."

"Would you want to marry me?"

"Yes." His voice sounded a little hoarse. "I would."

Sylvia thought, "He would!"

"Sylvia Miller." Sylvia said thoughtfully. "How does it sound?"

"It doesn't." He sounded abrupt. "We'll take a different last name."

"And yet you were surprised that I hated my first name. Here you go, hating your last! What kind of name shall we take?"

"I don't know." He tried to turn it into a joke. "A more suitable one. Miller isn't a horse-worthy name. A great horse with a great horse name would be... Princess Sylvia..."

He didn't get to finish.

"Princess, Grandma is calling for you!" It was Vince.

Sylvia had no idea that Vince was over.

They left the dock and headed for the house. Timothy was walking as though he was totally unaware of Vince's presence. Or, maybe, he didn't even notice Vince.

"See you tomorrow." Sylvia said.

Timothy stood still for a few moments looking at the door that closed behind her.

Vince was leaving, despite of all Grandma's efforts to persuade him to stay. Sylvia walked him out and he stopped in the doorway. "Listen, I'm sorry. I was so rude the other day. Remember? At the party. I don't even know what came over me."

She nodded.

He took her by the shoulders and looked in her eyes.

"Everything's gone haywire this summer, Princess. I don't know what's happening."

Timidly, he leaned in to kiss her. Sylvia raised her hand and held out her palm blocking her lips. He smiled gently and kissed her palm.

"Alright then, I better go."

She closed the door and listened for the sound of the engine running. Vince left.

Sylvia thought, "What was going on?" She herself had no idea about what was happening. For as long as she could remember, she always identified herself with Vince. Every summer the two of them were like one creature. A fun, spunky, loud and trouble-making creature. With double the energy, ideas and creativity. And every winter it wasn't that she would forget about Vince, it was just that his image would get buried deep down waiting for his time. Every spring she'd start to miss him. Impatiently, she'd wait around for the summer, making her eager plans.

She remembered he once asked, they were only about three or four years old, "Who are we, brother and sister, or husband and wife?" She knew for sure that they were no brother and sister. Because every summer all the cousins lived at Grandma's house, but Vince didn't. Then, were they husband and wife? She'd never doubted that was how it would be and never thought about it twice. She didn't get to see him last summer. And the summers before that they were still such kids. But the sparks had already begun to fly between the two of them. It felt like some vague expectation of something. That's why she was so looking forward to this summer and to their meeting again. So what was happening?

"Sweetheart..." Grandma sounded tired as she peeked into the hallway. "Why aren't you in bed yet? Is Vince gone already?"

Sylvia changed and pulled the blanket all the way up to her chin. She felt a strange chill. Grandma came in and sat down on the bed's edge. Sylvia shook off the blanket and wrapped herself around Grandma. So big, warm and dear, with the old familiar smell of their kitchen. Grandma hugged her granddaughter and patted her head as though she was a little girl. "What is the matter, sweetheart?"

"Grandma. I don't know what is happening to me."

"It's going to be okay. You'll see. Close your eyes and go to sleep. Tomorrow's a new day."

Grandma sighed and decided not to share her worries with Sylvia, the worries about Grandpa's poor health.

***

Timothy was back at his place.

Sylvia Miller. It's stupid, JK. But what was I supposed to do, tell her everything? I should, but it was just impossible.

Suddenly, he got an idea. He'd be better off writing to her. He had seen Sean store some note paper somewhere. Oh yeah, the boiler room!

He fished out a pack of yellow note paper stuffed between the old bills and record books. It took a while to locate a pencil. Finally, he sat down at the rough wooden table and sank into a deep thought. It turned out not to be so simple. He'd start, crumple up the paper and then start again.

It's impossible to express with words, JK!

As he finally figured out a way to express his feelings, things went a little easier. He forgot that he was even writing and didn't stop to think about words and expressions to use. It turned out to be a lot. He didn't re-read it. He shoved the letter into an envelope, threw the balled up sheets into the trash can, set them on fire, waited for the fire to die down and left with a lighter heart.

In the morning, Timothy got a mouthful from Sean about leaving the boiler room door open, "What could one possibly want there in the middle of night?"

"Sean, if something were to happen to me, would you please give this letter to Sylvia?" Timothy finally interrupted Sean.

"To Princess? Fine. And what can possibly happen to you?" Sean sounded surprised.

"Nothing. Then don't give it to her."

Sean mumbled something about Tim being crazy, and stuffed the envelope into the pocket of his old coat hanging on a nail on the boiler room door.

He's either going to lose it or forget all about it, JK. I guess it means nothing will happen. What is it with me? I'm just going to leave is all.

Early in the morning Vince showed up at his Uncle Jack's office.

"Why don't you take Sylvia for a ride someplace fun?" Uncle Jack was genuinely surprised.

Vince waved his hand.

"I should have gotten a job, just like last summer. There was no point in coming here."

"You're always fighting and making up." Jack smiled.

"Thing is... we didn't even fight. It's just... we each have separate lives now."

Uncle Jack smiled. Oh, the Prince and the Princess.

"It happens. Don't worry. A friendship like you two have doesn't just pass." He patted Vince's back, and gave him a load of work to do, since he was there anyway.

The phone rang. Forced to listen in against his will Vince waited till the conversation was finished to ask, "What's wrong with Tim Miller?"

"Everything's fine. Sylvia's Grandma was asking to get some information on him. You know, he's employed on their farm."

Uncle Jack decided to be discreet about the true cause for Grandma's worries.

"So I did. But a friend of mine took things a little too seriously and just called me with some new information. Just an insignificant detail. Last night Tim called his mother to tell her he was fine. It's been more than a month since she heard anything from him."

At first, Vince nodded indifferently, but then suddenly he jumped up, "He couldn't have called last night. I saw him - he never went inside the house!"

"They were hanging out on that darn dock all night. The dock that was only built there because of me, by the way."

"I guess he could have called earlier. There's a time difference."

"Is there anything else interesting about this Miller character?" Vince asked trying to sound indifferent.

"Nothing, really. He lost his driver's license about a month ago and got a new one, that's his only crime." His uncle laughed.

Vince got busy with the office work.

"Wait a minute. He was here a month ago. How could he get a driver's license elsewhere while being here?" Jack felt he had lost his fine touch having been in the boss's chair too long, though he used to be quite the detective back.

Vince quickly got bored with sealing envelopes and shifting papers about. And you call this police work? He decided to go over to the McGregor's farm. There should be some interesting work and help needed there. It would be even better to go over to Sylvia's. But no, she's got a new helper these days.

As soon as the door closed behind Vince, Uncle Jack took the receiver off the hook and dialed his friend's number.

***

Grandpa tossed and turned all night in pain. Completely exhausted by morning, Grandma told Sylvia, "You know what! Why don't you take the 'troublemakers' away to some place for the day? Grandpa's in a really bad shape and they are making way too much noise. Take Vince along."

One look at Sylvia was louder than words. Grandma sighed. "Fine. Take Tim along then, if you insist."

"If you're looking for Tim, he's probably still sleeping away." Sean said and started grumbling on and on about Tim's being like a different person lately, before he was up at the crack of dawn, and now he had to be woken up him, the guy had gotten too comfortable.

Sylvia turned beet red and thought, "When am I ever going to be rid of this childish habit of turning red for any small reason? What was the big deal about our spending time together every evening? We didn't do anything we would be embarrassed to talk about!"

Sure enough, Timothy was still asleep, his mouth open. Loudly, he sighed and shivered in his sleep. A few drops of perspiration were glistening on his forehead. Gently, Sylvia shook his shoulder. Suddenly she felt like running away. She thought, "Maybe, it really would have been a better idea to take Vince along?"

Timothy sat up abruptly and grabbed her by the hand.

"Oh, it's you." He looked visibly relieved.

Letting go of her hand he asked, "What time is it?"

Sylvia made a step back. "Seven A.M., sleepy head. We have an order from Grandma to take the 'troublemakers' away for the day."

"Where to?" He was blinking sleepily.

"I don't know."

Timothy was at last fully awake. He scratched the top of his head and shyly offered, "Maybe, to our beach?"

And she went to get ready.

"OUR beach! OUR beach!" She forgot all about how she just saw a stranger in a sleeping Timothy.

Timothy made sure that Sylvia was gone. He quickly got up and got ready.

What car should I take, JK? I bet this Gypsy character will be sure to tag along.

The 'troublemakers' behaved badly on the way there, yelling, fighting, and complaining about one another. Mark's heel landed on the back of Timothy's head, while he was wrestling some box out of Michael's hands and complaining, "I found it first yesterday!" Timothy lost all his patience, stopped the car and opened the door. "That's it. Get out of here!"

Gypsy King, in happy anticipation, stuck out his nose. Finally, here was freedom!

"Gypsy King, stay put! Did the rest of you hear me? Out of here! You can start walking home."

The troublesome threesome kept frightfully quiet.

"Fine, let's keep going then. But keep in mind, one more fight - you're out of the car and walking home, while Sylvia and I go swimming."

Frightened, the 'troublemakers' stayed quiet for a while, then got louder and louder as they were attempting to sneak one another a punch, while glancing with fear to make sure that Timothy wasn't looking. About an hour later, the car fell quiet. Surprised, Timothy glanced into the rearview mirror. "Check it out, they're all sleeping!"

"The car rocked them to sleep."

"I guess I'll have to charge double the price for today."

Their eyes met and they burst out laughing.

"Do you have babysitting experience?" Sylvia asked still smiling. "Or younger siblings?"

"What gives?"

"The way you've got them to mind was pretty clever!"

"Right. Except I kept thinking, what if they do leave the car and start running home?"

They exchanged smiling glances.

"But no, I never babysat. And I didn't have anybody but JK." Timothy answered her question. "Although if you count foals, then yes, I've spend my share with kids. Though foals are a bit calmer."

"Where did you see them?"

"I worked on a race track once. JK tracked down where in town they had some horses. We gave up washing cars and started visiting the track. All our free time we hung out there."

"How come you didn't get a recommendation letter from them for Grandma?"

Timothy sighed, then, quickly, came up with a response, "Why would I? I wasn't looking to make money; I just wanted to get some experience working the farm. I thought I would need different skills here anyway."

He fell quiet for a second.

"I really like it here."

"I'm glad you do. What was the racetrack like? Totally different probably?"

"Very different. The farm's a whole lot better." He thoughtfully went on explaining. "The horses are different here."

"Don't say so! Our horses have a ways to go compared to race horses!"

"How can I explain it to you?" He felt stumped for words to describe something he felt so deeply. "There it's like the epicenter of energy, excitement, the bustle of gambling. The people and the horses alike are strained with anticipation, with eagerness."

Sylvia looked at him with curiosity. She couldn't have expected such eloquence from the normally very quiet Timothy. His words breathed a new unknown world at her.

"And what about here?" She asked.

"Here? It's horse heaven!" He laughed. "And it's hard to say who's in charge here, the people or the horses. They run when they please and for their own pleasure."

"But if racing is in your blood, you must like to compete." Sylvia argued.

"Well, then all horses are exactly where they belong. I just prefer these kinds of horses."

"Yeah. All horses are where they belong." Sylvia declared with ease. "You know, it's the way Grandma decided to have it. She could have easily bred racehorses. But she doesn't feel like it. And I like it just this way anyhow."

***

A sleeping Martin kicked a sleeping Mark; the latter woke up and woke everyone around him. It was a good thing they were minutes away from the beach.

"It figures!" Sylvia sounded upset. "As soon as you bring a kite along, the wind dies down."

Stubborn 'troublemakers' were determined to launch it. The kite ended up in the water. Timothy dragged the soaked kite out to the shore and spread it out to dry on some bushes.

"It might look soaking wet and droopy, but it is nevertheless a proud flag of our Kingdom." Timothy said.

"You're so talkative today." Sylvia said tenderly.

She thought "OUR Kingdom!" and felt like she expected something more. She didn't know what exactly. More words, more actions. Something that would once again reaffirm their inner connection. Sylvia thought, "Why did he seem so different during the day than at night? Or was she the different one?"

The wind picked up after all. The 'troublemakers' lost control of the beach ball and it flew away over the water's edge along the shore. They raced after it, but the tricky wind kept grabbing the ball from right under their noses and kept moving it forward. Gypsy King ran silly circles around the 'troublemakers' instead of trying to help them get the ball. He was barking frantically demanding to know the meaning of this game.

Timothy jumped to his feet and ran after them. He was running with such easy grace that Sylvia couldn't keep her eyes off of him. He quickly caught the ball and jogged back.

"Here." He handed her the ball. "You'd better hide it or it'll end up in the lake. I don't want to dive after the troublemakers."

The boys tried to make peace with the ball being gone and decided to go build a sand castle instead. Gypsy Kind started digging a hole nearby. Martin threw his arms around the dog's body and tried to direct this live excavator to dig a tunnel around their castle.

"What are they, triplets?" Timothy asked.

"Michael and Mark are twins. Martin is their cousin."

"Funny, Martin and Michael look more alike." Timothy noted.

"Why not? Their fathers are twins. My uncles."

What a twisted family, JK.

Timothy caught himself wanting to ask how Gypsy King was related to them all.

"Grandma has three daughters and twin sons." Sylvia continued explaining as she sighed. "Oh, I'm so afraid!"

"Afraid of what?" Timothy was surprised.

"To give birth. What if I have twins?"

Timothy turned away trying to hide his smile.

"What about your Grandma? And these guys' mother?"

"Well, you are not the one who has to do it. And anyway. Men are much better off."

Sylvia felt the pangs of disappointment. He should have said "Don't worry, I'll be there!" Though why did she decide he should say any such thing? Gosh, everything was so complicated.

The 'troublemakers' buried Timothy in the sand. They kept trying to but couldn't get to a stopping point. An Egyptian pyramid made entirely out of sand towered over Timothy. The 'pharaoh' was shaking his head from side to side and squinting hard to keep the sand from getting into his eyes. Sylvia walked up and seated herself right next to him leaning back against the pyramid as though it was a back of a chair.

"Hey there!" The voice of the 'pharaoh' came from the other side. "How long do I have to lay here?"

Sylvia got on all fours and peeked around to see how he was doing. "They got you good, huh? You'd better stay put."

She reached out her hand and shook the sand out of his hair. His hair wasn't as soft and silky as Vince's. It was coarse. But she liked it. Thick and disobedient. She turned red and jerked her hand away.

"Alright, get up."

"Gotta eat!" Martin called.

"Gotta pee!" Michael said.

"Gotta drink!" Mark said.

"Come with me!" Timothy called to Michael and took him over to the brushwood.

"Wait! Let him put his sandals on!"

As he was walking, Michael was filling his sandals full of sand then dumping it all out. He heard some rustling in the bushes and took Timothy by the hand. Surprised, Timothy stared at him.

I have to get out of here, JK. Get. Out.

A seagull was desperately begging them for food, but it was afraid to get too close. Mark tossed her a piece of a banana.

"What are you doing? Seagulls don't eat that!" Sylvia retorted.

"Look! It did! It ate it up!"

Indeed, the seagull did eat the banana. It seemed to like it too. It got braver and approached them for more.

"Just look at it, what a gourmand!" Sylvia laughed.

"It could just be so hungry that it's ready to swallow whatever comes its way." Timothy offered.

"Did you mean to say so lazy? Or that there's a shortage of fish in the lake?"

"Let's settle on curious?" smiled Timothy.

"Agreed. Curious sounds good." And she exclaimed, "It's so good to be with you!" Embarrassed, she stopped.

***

The 'troublemakers' were peacefully asleep. Timothy caught sight of a furry family crossing the road. He gently slowed the car and parked it on the shoulder letting the 'pedestrians' pass.

"Raccoons." Sylvia smiled. "Good thing they weren't skunks!"

Timothy nodded in agreement.

It was dusk. Quietness settled in. There were few passing cars and not one was going in their direction.

They faced one another. Timothy drew Sylvia close, put his arms around her and kissed her. It was a long, long kiss. He let go and looked at her. Those eyes on her! Like a frightened foal. Timothy gave a deep sigh, started the engine and set off driving.

Sylvia thought, "Is that it? What a kiss it was! It was so... So wonderful! That's why there should have been at least two!"

That's it. I'm out of here tomorrow, JK. I'm all done here. Sean will give her the letter. The letter! Maybe, I shouldn't have written it? Oh well, it doesn't matter now. Starting tomorrow, I won't set my foot here again!

Sylvia thought, "What was wrong? Did I do something wrong? Why was he quiet? Maybe now he thought less of me. Maybe I shouldn't have responded to his kiss?"

The light went on inside the house. Grandma came out but before she got to saying anything, Sylvia signaled her to be quiet - Timothy was already out with one of the sleeping 'troublemakers' in his arms.

"Where to?" He whispered.

He took the sleeping child to bed and returned for the next one. Grandma kept following him and quietly going on and on about waking the boys and getting them washed up.

"Grandma, you'll wash them in the morning, alright?" Sylvia insisted.

She went to lock up behind Timothy and they both stopped in the doorway. He stepped from foot to foot and said:

"I have to go. I have some business to take care of and I'll be back."

He awkwardly ran his fingers along her cheek and left.

With a yawn, Sylvia was just heading to her room to get some sleep as she suddenly remembered. What did he just say? He is not coming back right now, tonight, is he?

The next day Timothy didn't leave as planned.

I'll get paid tomorrow or the day after and then leave, JK.

Of course, he could ask for an early pay but for some reason decided not to.

He saw Sylvia only briefly. Grandma sent her and the 'troublemakers' away for the day again but with Melissa this time. Out to the city.

Sylvia missed him and tried to imagine that Timothy was there with them. Except everything with him never turned out quite the way she imagined. Not better, not worse, just different. Maybe they'd get to spend some time by the river again tonight.

"What's with you?" Melissa sounded curious. "You've got a very mysterious smile going on there."

Sylvia hugged and kissed her. Melissa shook her head, having a good guess about what was going on.

"Both McDonald's and the movies!" The 'troublemakers' were demanding.

"Fine." Melissa gave a mischievous smile. "But first we go shopping and you don't get to make a single sound!"

A police car arrived in the evening, just as Sylvia returned back from the city, and she saw Timothy being taken away.

If only he had looked at her. Guiltily. Or reassuringly. But not even a glance her way.

"He had a fake ID on him! He is not Tim Miller!" Melanie reported excitedly.

"So who is he?"

"Nobody knows. And he won't say a word!"

"That doesn't mean anything!" Sylvia yelled out. "So what he found an ID and used it to get a job here with the horses!"

"Oh yeah?" Melanie wasn't backing down. "So how did he know that Grandma hired Tim Miller? And why didn't he use his real name?"

"Maybe he murdered the real Tim Miller." Melinda suggested almost dreamily.

"Shut up!" Melissa said.

"The real Tim Miller who's still alive called home the other day and said that he was just fine." Grandma informed them glancing worriedly at Sylvia.

"And what did he say?" Melanie was just dying from curiosity.

"Who?" Grandma seemed confused.

"The real Tim Miller. Did he lose his ID?"

"I don't know. They haven't located him yet."

"Jack's got a big mouth." All Grandpa could do was shake his head. "He doesn't belong in my former position."

"Well, what if Tim Miller is indeed dead? And they just played an old voice recording over the phone?" Melinda wouldn't leave it.

"Keep reading those detective novels." Melissa cut her off. "Only in those can somebody talk to a voice recording and not notice a thing."

Sylvia got up and went upstairs.

"You idiots!" Melissa addressed her cousins. "Are you blind? Stop torturing our Princess!"

Grandma followed Sylvia upstairs. Her granddaughter was laying on the bed her face in the pillow.

"Come here." Grandma's arms were around her. "My sweet baby."

Sylvia cuddled up to her Grandma and whispered. "Grandma, he couldn't have done anything wrong. He's a good guy, Grandma. He is so wonderful; he doesn't even like race horses."

Though Grandma didn't understand a thing, she comforted Sylvia the best she could, "It's okay. The police will figure it out. Everything's going to be all right."

She sat with Sylvia a little while and had to go feed the 'troublemakers' frustrated over not having figured out things about this Tim Miller earlier. Grandma thought, "We shouldn't have hired help to begin with. Poor Princess. I'll call Vince tomorrow. He's so diplomatic. He'll know exactly what to do to distract Sylvia. Soon enough she'll forget everything."

    ***

"Well, Grandma, tell us! Why aren't they letting him go all this time?" Melanie begged.

Grandma shook her head. Four pairs of eyes stared at her expectantly. Sylvia got up, sighed and took Grandma's hand.

"Alright." Grandma gave in. "They found the real Tim Miller. He called his mother again. He says he lost his driver's license and has never seen the fake Tim Miller ("Timothy." Sylvia silently corrected her) in his life. Our ("Our." Echoed in Sylvia's head) Tim keeps silent and refuses to name himself. He insists that he found the driver's license. He says he overheard Tim Miller talk to somebody at a rest stop, but he doesn't remember where. The real Tim was saying that he had to go to the farm but changed his mind."

"He stole the driver's license!" Melanie concluded.

Once their curiosity was satisfied, the girls went about their business. They remembered to stop themselves from discussing the news in Sylvia's presence.

"Well," When Grandpa was finally left alone with Grandma his voice had a hint of irony. "What did Jack blabber to you this time?"

"What do you expect? I did employ this Tim Miller! So I have every right to know!" Grandma defended herself. "I am an interested party."

"Fine, fine. Spill it. What else did you find out?"

"The motorcycle. The motorcycle belongs to the real Tim Miller. And he also has a large sum of money."

"Which one does?" Sylvia gasped.

"The real one." Grandma turned to face her. "Since when have you started eavesdropping?"

"I'm just listening. I'm also an interested party. Don't you think so?"

"Sylvia, if you know something, something that can shed the light on this story, please tell us." Grandpa asked gently.

Sylvia shook her head. "Nothing at all."

She locked her door and fell onto her bed. Sylvia thought, "Of course, I know something. Timothy didn't lie to me. Never. He just wasn't telling everything. There was something he couldn't tell EVEN to me. Timothy couldn't have done anything bad. He wasn't like that! He was so gentle and shy. He was the best one in the whole world. They couldn't keep him there forever. Sooner or later they would have to let him go. It couldn't be a crime to hide your real name, could it? Timothy. A cousin nicknamed J.K. Born in Eastern Europe. He lived in a big city different from Toronto. It had a racetrack. It had to be in the States, not in Canada. That was a fact. If the police needed to, they could find out for themselves. Why should I tell them if he wouldn't? Timothy, Timothy, Timothy."

In her mind, Sylvia was sorting through each of their encounters, laughing and crying at the same time. "Miller isn't a horse-worthy name. I was so selfish! If only I had pressed him a little back, then he would have told me everything and together we would have figured out what to do. Women sometimes are, if not more intelligent, then definitely more inventive than men! He was stuck here because of me!"

Now she got it. "Back then he wanted to leave. That's what he was trying to tell me. And he didn't leave. Timothy..." Sylvia thought. "What if he did do something awful? And... then kissed me? No. Not him. He couldn't have."

For some reason she remembered his jogging with the beach ball in his hands. He was smiling so wide but then the smile slowly faded. Sylvia thought, "Oops, and we forgot our kite in the bushes. A wet and droopy flag of OUR kingdom." She didn't just sob - she howled covering her mouth with a pillow.

"Sylvia, open up!" Grandma was knocking on her door.

Sylvia didn't open. Grandma sighed and left.

"What have I done? How could I let this happen? Who could have known? My poor Princess."

"It's hard without Tim around." Sean said to Grandma. "It's like I'm missing an arm. Are they letting him go soon?"

"I don't know. I don't know anything these days." That was the only answer Grandma could offer. She thought, "It would be better if he didn't return. It would be even better if he never showed up here to begin with. We'll get through. Time will heal."

***

"Sean! Sean! I've got a bill for the oats again. Haven't we paid it already?" Grandma asked.

"I can't remember." Sean said. "Let me go check."

He grabbed the bill and headed for the boiler room. He found the needed note in the record book. Sean thought, "What do they think billing them twice, they think we won't notice! Though who knows these young people these days, so empty-headed, they probably forgot and sent the bill again."

Sean got up from the desk and saw an envelope sticking out of his old jacket's pocket. He thought, "Oh shoot! I am forgetting things myself. Tim asked me to give this to Princess. Should I or should I wait till he's back? I'd better give it to her, it won't make matters worse."

Sylvia practically grabbed the envelope from of his hands and ran. Her fingers were trembling as she was opening it.

Dear Sylvia!

If you're reading this letter, it means I'm either on the run or no longer alive.

I don't want to get all of you involved in this business. I borrowed this suspense novel from Sean once - it was so dumb - good enough for putting you to sleep. But there was one thing it said I did like: "don't endanger those you love." That's why I decided to leave. And I have to explain why.

JK and his folks moved to another city. They shouldn't have. Things were bad for him there from the start. He called once and said that we needed to talk. When I went to meet JK, the bus was a half hour late. Had it arrived on time, JK would still be alive.

The scariest part is that if the bus was only fifteen minutes late, I would have seen JK falling down with my own eyes. I often dream of catching him as he falls. It's better when I dream him still alive. Or that I get there on time. Or that all this is a terrible mistake. Or he falls, but still makes it.

*Police documented it as a "narcotic intoxication." **He fell out of the window** or, maybe, jumped out. JK couldn't have, he just couldn't have. Even if on drugs. Except nobody wanted to listen to me.*

The police officer said we understand, he's your relative, we are sorry for your loss, you have to go on living for him. That's it. They were not even going to investigate what happened to JK.

I kept telling them that JK was expecting me. He couldn't have bought the beer, ordered pizza (the kind he and I always liked, whom else would he have ordered that many anchovies for?), opened the window and jumped out to greet me. Nonsense.

They said, "Drugs, it happens all the time".

JK's father was sitting and crying. I stayed with them for a while, my parents didn't mind. JK's parents moved to a different apartment, they couldn't stay in the old one.

The first thing I did was to find the closest race track. Yes, JK worked here even though it was a little out of the way. Where else could he have found horses in the city? I got a job there too. I didn't tell them JK and I were related. I didn't want to hear empty sympathies. So I started watching and asking questions. They got JK involved in such a mess. Sylvia, you're better off not knowing the whole story. The drugs weren't even the main thing. I was shaking with anger. My hands trembled all the time. Looking back I can't believe how calmly I could act.

I can't even imagine what they are going to tell you about me. It's best if you hear it from me first. So, you don't think badly of me, or JK. I was so miserable over what they'd done to him, I could have killed them with my bare hands. I knew who to kill, people like that gang have no business being near horses.

The owners liked me and trusted me. Once I found an incriminating letter. Only because I kept looking for something all the time, I didn't even know what for exactly. This idea hit me that if I removed the postscript, the meaning of the letter would be changed. I was looking for a payback and this was a perfect opportunity to sabotage Boldie. I cut off the bottom of the letter. I put it back where I found it.

The Boss shot Boldie in the stables. The shot didn't sound real. It didn't even frighten the horses. The Boss didn't see me and left. I went and looked. Boldie was deader than dead. He was such an animal.

Boldie's brother, or whatever they were, shot the Boss, Boss's men then shot Boldie's brother. All three deaths were my responsibility. Murderer. It's as though I pulled the trigger myself. I couldn't sleep at night until I ended up on your farm.

It was stupid of me not to get out of there right away. Someone saw me. They told the new boss that I was living at JK's parents. He put two and two together.

I wish it was not me but the police who found out that it was Boldie leaving JK's place that day. But they couldn't have cared less. Boldie pushed him out. It was clear as daylight. Boss got fed up with JK and they did away with him. JK could go overboard easily but not when it came to the horses.

I made a bet. I worked at the race course half my life and never bet but that day I did. I took what I won and left. I don't know why they didn't kill me. They had plenty of chances. Either they wanted to find something out from me or just thought I would always be there. They didn't expect me to run away. I don't know. They lost me near the Canadian border. At a rest stop, across the border this hairy hippie guy named Tim Miller joined me at the table and we got to talking. I mean he did. He complained that he was so desperate to get out of his house that he stupidly found a job on a horse farm. And I said I would even pay extra just to get to work on a horse farm, I loved horses. He laughed and asked how much I'd be willing to pay. I made an offer. He took the bait. He said they were expecting him and might not want to hire me. He said I must be joking to offer that much - I wouldn't make that much working there all summer, why do you need it?

I guess, you're right, I said. Maybe, you'll throw your motorcycle in for cheap, I've wanted one like that my whole life. How would I get there otherwise having no money? The motorcycle sealed the deal; he asked double the price for it.

I told him what if I said I lost my ID and they would be asking questions, it would be better to have one. We agreed that he would give me his driver's license but wouldn't get another one right away. He was so happy he even left me his stuff. I went and buried my documents.

I thought it might get complicated since he was three years older and we looked nothing alike. At least our first names nearly matched.

I tried not to think about that pack of wolves, tried to forget them. If I didn't think about it I could pretend they'd never find me. But the police could find me. My parents could realize I was missing and start looking. I don't trust the police. They are so indifferent, they couldn't care less about JK. They'd throw me to the wolves just the same.

And then you came. And that was it. It's better if I leave. Forgive me, if you can.

Timothy.

The tears were practically choking Sylvia. Grandma knocked on the door. Sylvia opened it wide.

"Grandma, is he still alive?"

"Of course he is, what are you saying!"

"Have they let him go?"

"No, they took him to Toronto."

"Why?"

"They've got some information from Vancouver. They are trying to see if they can identify him. Sylvia, Sean told me that you've got some sort of a letter. Baby girl, it would be best if you tell us what's going on." Grandma said with a sick feeling in her stomach. She knew there was a reason she didn't like that Tim from the start.

"No, Grandma, they'll kill him. Don't you understand? If he's not saying anything, there must be a reason for it?"

But a feeling of doubt crept in. Sylvia felt she needed advice.

"Grandma, if I tell you, will you swear not to tell anyone?"

"No." Grandma shook her head. "This is so serious I can't keep it from Grandpa."

Sylvia sat down on the bed and clutched the letter to her chest. She hesitated. How could she help so that she wouldn't make it worse?

"Fine. Let's go see Grandpa."

"Grandpa, I need some advice. Somebody's life is on the line." Sylvia collected all her strength and continued. "I think that he's not acting in his best interests, but I don't want anything to be done without his agreement."

***

Timothy raised his head in surprise.

Isn't it, what's his name, Uncle Jack? What's he doing here, JK?

"Listen to me, young fellow. There's a document. I know what it contains, but I gave my word to the owner of the document not to use the information without your agreement. And I'm going to keep my word."

Slowly Timothy was figuring out what he was talking about.

"Sooner or later you'll be identified and you'll get kicked out of Canada and go home. Don't you want to get this to its logical conclusion and put those criminals behind bars?"

"I don't believe you. You couldn't care less about them. And you couldn't care less about me."

Jack paused. Then he smiled.

"Then what were you doing courting a former police officer's granddaughter?"

"What?" Timothy looked at Uncle Jack in disbelief. "Grandpa?"

"A former chief of the local police department."

Timothy smiled ironically.

What a family, JK.

"Let me tell you what safety guarantees are offered to you by the American side. What is needed from the witness. Then you can tell me your opinion."

It's not like I'm worried for myself, JK.

Timothy shrugged. But for just a moment his face changed as though he was hit by a sharp pain. Suddenly, Uncle Jack realized what was going on with him. His sympathized with the guy.

"You have nothing to blame yourself for."

"If only." Timothy's voice sounded course. "I murdered them. It's as good as if it was me. And I wanted it to happen."

Even if they were the worst monsters on the planet, I didn't have a right to do it, not even for you, JK.

"And now... I..." Timothy whispered and didn't finish, trying to keep himself from crying.

Uncle Jack grabbed a chair and sat down thinking hard about the words to use for a conversation that would take a while.

     ***

"For the purposes of the investigation all information remains confidential," said Uncle Jack. "Forget all you ever knew. There was a Tim Miller. Who he turned out to be is unknown. They took him away. What, who, where - you are not aware."

Sylvia nodded and asked, "Can I see him?"

"No. Not until the investigation is over. In any case, he's probably already been taken to the States."

Sylvia got up her head hanging low. Grandma felt so bad for her.

"By the way, he asked me to tell you something about a horse name." Uncle Jack remembered.

"What about it?" Sylvia turned around sharply.

"Something like..." Uncle Jack tried to remember the strange message. "Something about there being a name for some horse, a last name. No, that's not it. Great horse and she needs a name? I can't remember. It makes no sense."

Sylvia smiled happily.

On the way home Grandma couldn't wait and asked. "So what does all this talk about a horse name mean?"

"It means..." Sylvia was laughing. "That Timothy loves me. Something like that."

"Oh God, how could there be love?" Grandma was thinking to herself. "It's okay, time will pass and everything will be forgotten. Vince will get here tomorrow, and the McGregors invited us out for tomorrow. This will remain only a memory. An adventure of youth."

In the evening Sylvia was feeling down again. She was worried about what her Grandpa told her regarding how long an investigation might take. She couldn't have imagined that it might take that long. Besides, Grandpa says that the investigation would not be the end.

"Princess, could you go turn the pot off in the kitchen?" Grandma asked her.

The water in the pot boiled over and put out the pilot light. Sylvia thought she was just in time. And suddenly she remembered a story Timothy told her.

Once, JK and he were bored. They were sitting at home doing nothing. They got this idea to make balloons fly. They used their gas-stove to inflate the balloons. For some reason the balloons weren't flying. It was a good thing JK's dad woke up. He nearly died when he saw what was happening, so he turned on the vent. He got so scared that he forgot to punish them. She was laughing at the story back then on the dock imagining small guys like the 'troublemakers' in the kitchen full of balloons and in walks a father. Sylvia put her face in her hands and started sobbing. Her heart was breaking from the sorrow she felt for Timothy, for JK, for herself. That was how Grandma found her.

One day, all the young people got two cars and went to the beach that Sylvia and Timothy discovered. The weather was great. Eric suggested going for a swim and the 'troublemakers' just begged to go to the old place. It took them not three, but a whole four hours to get there for some reason, so they never went to that beach again. It seemed too far, Wasaga Beach was much closer. And nobody liked how isolated the beach was and how wild it was around. The sand pyramid built by the 'troublemakers' over the 'pharaoh' still towered over the water. Sylvia sat down at its bottom, leaned back and closed her eyes.

A beach ball flew her way. Vince came up and stretched out his hand:

"Get up, let's go play."

She shook her head no.

There was no news from Timothy.

Grandma watched her granddaughter jump up with every phone call or sound, running to the door at any sound of someone knocking, and she was suffering alongside Sylvia but thought, "It's okay. She'll go home soon and forget about everything." As if in a silent agreement, no one said a word about anything to Sylvia's parents.

Soon all the grandkids left. Sylvia was the last one to leave and reluctantly at that. The house emptied out for the winter.

Epilogue

"Let me out here." Timothy asked the driver.

The truck stopped.

Timothy jumped out onto the ground.

What if I'm not welcome?

The truck left. Timothy collected his courage and headed for the porch.

In the yard he ran into Melissa.

"Tim!" She clasped her hands and gave a deafening yell. "Sylvia! Look who's here!"

Definitely, no one talks quietly in this house.

He was nearly knocked to the ground by a golden-fur tornado. Timothy threw his backpack onto the ground. Bent down and patted the dog on the head with his hand:

"Gypsy King! My boy! You recognized me! Good dog!"

Gypsy King wagged his tail and whimpered happily trying hard to lick the Timothy's hand.

Timothy straightened up, turned and saw Sylvia right in front of him. He hadn't heard her approach. His heart stopped beating. But Sylvia just stared without a blink. Without a smile.

"I'm back." Timothy stammered shyly.

She started crying without a sound. He felt lost.

"Why did it take you so long?" Sylvia asked sternly.

"I came as soon as I could. It's true."

Sylvia snuffled and wiped her tears.

"I was waiting for you. That's all. It was awful. I can't even remember what this year was like."

"So, you won't even tell me any news?" He was still feeling awkward.

She started telling the news and it calmed her down.

"Grandpa's back is so bad he barely ever walks. Melinda is getting married. To Eric. The wedding is this fall."

"Melinda is? Not Melissa?" He smiled.

"Can you imagine? We didn't expect it either. Grandma says that Melissa is too picky."

They both laughed.

"Bird died. He got bitten by a fox."

"Poor Bird." Timothy touched her arm.

Then he said, nearly whispering, "Keep on telling."

However, she didn't manage to get anything else out. Gypsy King swirled around them, sniffed the backpack and started tearing it with his teeth. Timothy took the "prey" away and threatened Gypsy King with this fist.

"I missed you so much." Sylvia sighed. "I came here as soon as school was out, I didn't even stay for the prom. I was afraid to miss you."

"And see, I missed your birthday." He sounded disappointed.

All three cousins were out on the porch watching the reunion. Out came Grandma. She stared for a second and with great surprise realizing it was Timothy she yelled out. "And who is our visitor? Come on into the house!"

Timothy shook the hand of Grandpa who was now in a wheelchair but still looked cheerfully at the world. That's why they paved the yard, Grandpa's moving around on wheels now.

"Well, hero. Do tell us everything!" said Grandpa.

"Wait a minute, he just arrived." Grandma interrupted him and asked Timothy. "Would you like some lunch?"

"Yes please." Timothy answered.

"He's still gulping food down without chewing." Grandma thought to herself. "But at least his hands seem clean now."

"Did you hire any help this year yet?" Timothy pulled away from the plate. Melissa laughed.

"No way! After you, Grandma is scared of strangers. Sean is on his own."

"How's he doing?"

"He talks about you often. Eric helps him out once in a while."

"So are you going to tell us any details?" Melanie asked.

"Melanie!" Grandma snapped at her

"What?! So tell us, are you in the witness protection program? What really happened to your friend? What..."

"Melanie!" Grandma had had enough.

Sylvia was kneeling on the floor near the backpack and watched Timothy chew from down below.

"Take it out, there's a gift for you in there." He nodded at the backpack.

"What is this? Are these coins? Are they real? So thin? Timothy, are they real?" A beautiful gypsy necklace sparkled and jingled in her hands. "Where did you get it?"

Sylvia jumped on her feet, put on the necklace and started twirling around. Her foot knocked the backpack and a little box fell from its pocket. Sylvia kneeled again. Curious she opened the box. The cousins gasped.

"A ring?" Sylvia was dumbfounded. "Who is this for?"

"For you." Timothy said.

"Oh no." Melinda said. "You ruined your moment. Put it back and forget that you ever saw it!"

"Do you mean I can wear it?" Asked Sylvia not hearing anything.

"If you say Yes." Timothy said.

Sylvia put the ring on, stretched her hand forward and stared at her finger in surprise.

"Did you tell your parents where you went?" Grandpa asked.

"Didn't get to. I came here right away."

"Alright, why don't you call home then, so they won't worry?"

Timothy finished talking to his parents and put down the receiver.

"So are they aware that you decided to get married?" Melissa asked sarcastically.

"Not yet." Timothy answered calmly. "One step at a time. I'll tell them tomorrow."

"Can I go see the horses?" Timothy turned to Grandma.

"Sure." She was still in disbelief over his return.

Sylvia took Timothy's hand and they walked out.

"And what does all this mean?" Grandma asked.

"Tim just proposed and Sylvia accepted!" Melissa laughed.

"Our times are so complicated that it takes a marriage proposal for a man to prove his love!" Melanie all-knowingly raised her finger.

The cousins burst into laughter.

"I don't understand." Grandma said suddenly feeling ill when she realized that all laughter aside - the matter was quite serious. "And when are they getting married?"

"I think they are ready. Maybe even tomorrow!" Melissa smiled.

"It's true. Marriage can either make a man or break a man!" Melanie said theatrically.

"It can happen to a man without any marriage! If he's dating Melissa!" Melinda laughed.

"What an idiot she is, what's the rush?" Melissa let the joke go right over her head. "And then it will be too late. She'll already be married."

"I think she's lucky. It's so romantic. So intense. She was so heart-broken. And a proposal right off the bat. It's too bad she saw the ring too soon." Melanie said.

"What was intense?" Melissa wasn't giving in. "First guy she comes across. I've had a ton of guys like that! They'll run after me with marriage proposals if I so much as move my finger. Bo-ring! I'll find one who'll be worth getting married to. I'm not giving in so easily!"

"Is this really happening? Are the girls right?" Grandma sounded bewildered.

"It sounds like it is." Grandpa said.

"And what are we supposed to do?"

"What can we do? Look. It's just like you always wanted. If not your kids, then your grandkids are coming back to your nest, to your horses."

"Gosh, what am I going to tell my daughter?" Grandma could sense the difficult conversation with Sylvia's parents and she was getting ready to defend her granddaughter from her daughter. Grandpa, as always, would pass the difficult conversation to her shoulders. He'd remain the good guy. She would, as always, be the one to blame.

Sylvia leaned her shoulder against the wall and smiled as she watched Timothy making his rounds with the horses. Her fingers jingled the necklace. He said it was a fake. He had found it at a shop selling theatrical props. But she loved it. It jingled like... a harness. Sylvia laughed quietly.

"Does Sean know that Emperor's Death has something going on with her leg?" He turned to her with a look of worry on his face.

Some names they give around here.

"He does. The vet is supposed to be here tomorrow."

With great joy, Timothy inhaled the smells of the stables, turned to Sylvia and put his arms around her.

"So what is your last name?" She asked.

"Dubrowski. Timothy Dubrowski. Do you think it's worthy of one beautiful horse?" He smiled.

"Sylvia Dubrowski..." She tried it out and nodded in approval.

He kissed her. And then he did it again and again...

Made in the USA
Middletown, DE
30 October 2020